THE
JOURNEY
PRIZE

STORIES

WINNERS OF THE $10,000 JOURNEY PRIZE

1989: Holley Rubinsky for "Rapid Transits"

1990: Cynthia Flood for "My Father Took a Cake to France"

1991: Yann Martel for "The Facts Behind the Helsinki Roccamatios"

1992: Rozena Maart for "No Rosa, No District Six"

1993: Gayla Reid for "Sister Doyle's Men"

1994: Melissa Hardy for "Long Man the River"

1995: Kathryn Woodward for "Of Marranos and Gilded Angels"

1996: Elyse Gasco for "Can You Wave Bye Bye, Baby?"

1997 (shared): Gabriella Goliger for "Maladies of the Inner Ear"
                Anne Simpson for "Dreaming Snow"

1998: John Brooke for "The Finer Points of Apples"

1999: Alissa York for "The Back of the Bear's Mouth"

2000: Timothy Taylor for "Doves of Townsend"

2001: Kevin Armstrong for "The Cane Field"

2002: Jocelyn Brown for "Miss Canada"

2003: Jessica Grant for "My Husband's Jump"

2004: Devin Krukoff for "The Last Spark"

2005: Matt Shaw for "Matchbook for a Mother's Hair"

2006: Heather Birrell for "BriannaSusannaAlana"

2007: Craig Boyko for "OZY"

2008: Saleema Nawaz for "My Three Girls"

2009: Yasuko Thanh for "Floating Like the Dead"

2010: Devon Code for "Uncle Oscar"

2011: Miranda Hill for "Petitions to Saint Chronic"

2012: Alex Pugsley for "Crisis on Earth-X"

2013: Naben Ruthnum for "Cinema Rex"

2014: Tyler Keevil for "Sealskin"

2015: Deirdre Dore for "The Wise Baby"

2016: Colette Langlois for "The Emigrants"

2017: Sharon Bala for "Butter Tea at Starbucks"

2018: Shashi Bhat for "Mute"

The BEST of CANADA'S NEW WRITERS

THE

JOURNEY

PRIZE

STORIES

SELECTED BY

CARLEIGH BAKER

CATHERINE HERNANDEZ

JOSHUA WHITEHEAD

McCLELLAND & STEWART

Library and Archives Canada Cataloguing in Publication is available
upon request

Published simultaneously in the United States of America by
McClelland & Stewart, a Penguin Random House Company

Library of Congress Control Number is available upon request

ISBN: 978-0-7710-5079-4
ebook ISBN: 978-0-7710-5082-4

Cover design by Fernanda Oliveira
Typeset in Janson by M&S, Toronto
Printed and bound in Canada

McClelland & Stewart,
a division of Penguin Random House Canada Limited,
a Penguin Random House Company
www.penguinrandomhouse.ca

1 2 3 4 5   23 22 21 20 19

Penguin
Random House
McCLELLAND & STEWART

ABOUT THE JOURNEY PRIZE STORIES

The $10,000 Journey Prize is awarded annually to an emerging writer of distinction. This award, now in its thirty-first year, and given for the nineteenth time in association with the Writers' Trust of Canada as the Writers' Trust of Canada/McClelland & Stewart Journey Prize, is made possible by James A. Michener's generous donation of his Canadian royalty earnings from his novel *Journey*, published by McClelland & Stewart in 1988. The Journey Prize itself is the most significant monetary award given in Canada to a developing writer for a short story or excerpt from a fiction work in progress. The winner of this year's Journey Prize will be selected from among the twelve stories in this book.

The Journey Prize Stories has established itself as the most prestigious annual fiction anthology in the country, introducing readers to the finest new literary writers from coast to coast for three decades. It has become a who's who of up-and-coming writers, and many of the authors who have appeared in the anthology's pages have gone on to distinguish themselves with short story collections, novels, and literary awards. The anthology comprises a selection from submissions made by the editors of literary journals and annual anthologies from across the country, who have chosen what, in their view, is the most exciting writing in English that they have published in the previous year. In recognition of the vital role journals play in fostering literary voices, McClelland & Stewart makes its own award of $2,000 to the journal or anthology that originally published and submitted the winning entry.

This year the selection jury comprised three acclaimed writers:

Carleigh Baker is an nêhiyaw âpihtawikosisân/Icelandic writer who lives as a guest on the unceded territories of the xʷməθkʷəy̓əm, Skwxwu7mesh, and səl̓ilwəta peoples. Her work has appeared in *Best Canadian Essays*, *The Short Story Advent Calendar*, and *The Journey Prize Stories*. She also writes reviews for the *Globe and Mail* and the *Literary Review of Canada*. Her debut story collection, *Bad Endings* (Anvil), won the City of Vancouver Book Award, and was a finalist for the Rogers Writers' Trust Fiction Prize, the Indigenous Voices Award for Most Significant Work of Prose in English, and the BC Book Prize Bill Duthie Booksellers' Choice Award. She is the 2019/20 Writer in Residence at Simon Fraser University.

Catherine Hernandez is the Artistic Director of b current performing arts and the award-winning author of *Scarborough* (Arsenal Pulp Press). *Scarborough* won the 2015 Jim Wong-Chu Emerging Writers Award, was shortlisted for the Toronto Book Award, the Forest of Reading Evergreen Award, the Edmund White Award for Debut Fiction, and the Trillium Book Award, and longlisted for Canada Reads 2018. It made the "Best of 2017" lists for the *Globe and Mail*, *National Post*, *Quill and Quire*, and CBC Books. *Scarborough* will be adapted into a film by Compy Films, Reel Asian Film Festival, and Telefilm, with Catherine authoring the screenplay. She is currently working on her second and third books, *Crosshairs* and *PSW*, both forthcoming from HarperCollins Canada.

Joshua Whitehead is an Oji-Cree/nehiyaw, Two-Spirit/Indigiqueer member of Peguis First Nation (Treaty 1). His first novel, *Jonny Appleseed* (Arsenal Pulp Press), won a Lambda

Literary Award in Gay Fiction and the Georges Bugnet Award, was shortlisted for such prizes as a Governor General's Literary Award, the Amazon Canada First Novel Award, the Carol Shields City of Winnipeg Book Award, and the Firecracker Award, and was longlisted for the Scotiabank Giller Prize. He is also the author of the poetry collection *full-metal indigiqueer* (Talonbooks), which was shortlisted for the inaugural Indigenous Voices Award for Most Significant Work of Poetry in English and the Stephan G. Stephansson Award for Poetry. Currently, he is working on a Ph.D. in Indigenous Literatures and Cultures at the University of Calgary's English department (Treaty 7).

The jury read a total of ninety submissions without knowing the names of the authors or those of the publications in which the stories originally appeared. McClelland & Stewart would like to thank the jury for their efforts in selecting this year's anthology and, ultimately, the winner of this year's Journey Prize.

McClelland & Stewart would also like to acknowledge the continuing enthusiastic support of writers, literary editors, and the public in the common celebration of new voices in Canadian fiction.

For more information about *The Journey Prize Stories*, please visit www.facebook.com/TheJourneyPrize.

CONTENTS

KAI CONRADI

EVERY TRUE ARTIST

The sun has slipped behind the low-slung mountains by the time Yula pulls up at the motel, hands the driver a ten, and steps out onto the dirt. The desert sky stretches on, flat and colossal, so far that it hurts her eyes when she tries to take in where it begins or ends. On a cloudless night like this, the light fades quick. There is no sunset like she knows from Canada, where the clouds take on the last rays as golden, then pink, then purple—holding the dregs of light long after the sun has vanished. Here, night falls like the big cedar her brother, Rich, felled on their property last winter, and the spiny plants that stud the landscape become black and jagged.

The motel is a long, flat building of white brick, punctuated by nine doors—eight guest suites and a lobby. Across the street, a derelict gas station slouches into the dry earth. The motel sits on the highway that passes straight through the middle of Angel City, a town of less than a thousand inhabitants, composed—as far as she can tell—of rundown trailers and chain-link fences and backyards crammed with old furniture. Tied up in front of one of these trailers, a little ways down the road, several dogs bark. Their barking rattles around in the night like tin cans kicked down a street. A woman in jeans and a denim shirt emerges from the trailer and shouts at the dogs; kibble clatters against metal and the dogs jostle one another for their supper. From somewhere in the dark: Johnny Cash's "Green Green Grass of Home."

The sudden desert night chills Yula through her turtleneck and slacks. She picks up her suitcase and heads toward the warm light of the lobby. As she opens the plate glass door, it clangs against a silver spur that dangles from the doorframe. The walls of the lobby are a pale, dentist's-office green. A crooked, hand-painted border of pink roses runs along the walls, just below the ceiling, and all along it hang framed portraits of cowboys, most cut from magazines, their edges asymmetrical and sloppy. Behind the front desk sits a woman in a yellow western shirt patterned with tiny red horseshoes. Her large breasts hang low on her chest and push against the mother-of-pearl snaps that struggle to hold together the halves of the fabric. She wears oversized, green-rimmed glasses, and when she looks up at Yula her brown eyes are magnified to the size of walnuts. There is a large mole on her neck and another above her right eyebrow. Her name tag reads "Doreen." Doreen greets Yula and her voice is deep. Her open lips reveal gums packed with twice as many teeth as seem necessary on a human being.

You didn't see Ribs out there, did you? Doreen asks. She is younger than Yula—mid-to-late forties—and far from conventionally attractive. Her cherry-coloured hair—home-dyed, Yula hopes, for the woman's sake—drapes lank over her shoulders, and her face has an unimpressed, sagging quality that reminds Yula of a bloodhound. And yet, Yula bets that men would fight each other for this woman. It must be the way she looks at you: a total ambivalence that makes you want, more than anything, for her to care about you.

Ribs? Yula says. Is that a dog? She thinks of the dogs scrabbling on the dirt for their dinner. I'm here for the artist's residency, actually, she says. I'm Yula Curtain. I was supposed to be here this afternoon, but we had to make an emergency landing in Tomahawk because a woman was having a panic attack.

No part of Doreen's face displays interest at this information. Ribs is my boyfriend, she says. He rode his motorcycle over to Sasko last night, but we're going for steak tonight at Lou Harvey's.

She opens a drawer in her desk and, eyes still fixed on Yula, rummages her hand around in it. Yula looks at her feet. Already, her white Keds knock-offs have taken on a dust-brown. After a few minutes of half-hearted rummaging, Doreen pulls a plastic cactus keychain from the drawer. On it are two keys. One's for your room, she says, the other's for the ice machine around back. Make sure you don't leave the doors open or the scorpions will get in. And don't leave your shoes outdoors neither. You're room six. She gestures to the left. If you're gonna smoke in the room, make sure you don't burn the carpets or nothin', or I'll have to charge you for damage.

I don't smoke, says Yula. She takes the keys and tries to pocket them, but the pockets of her slacks are just for show. Do you know when Mr. Carver will show up? she asks.

That who you're sharing the room with? says the woman.

No, says Yula. Wince Carver, the man who runs the residency. She pulls at the bottom of her turtleneck, where it likes to ride up over her paunch.

The woman laughs a deep laugh, like rocks knocking together under the ocean, but her face remains flat. Good thing he's not your man, she says, 'cause the bed in room six is made for a scarecrow. You two'd have to lie on top of each other like those Dr. Seuss turtles. Her laughter stops and she looks bored. Anyway, I've got no idea, hun. I just work the front desk.

Yula turns to go and the front-desk woman adds, I'm here all day, by the way. Holler if you need anything. Oh, and if you smoke in your room, don't fall asleep with one in your mouth. Room six doesn't have a fire extinguisher and the local firetruck broke down two weeks ago and still ain't fixed.

All night, the fan in Yula's room whirrs. There doesn't appear to be an off switch, and she sleeps a fitful sleep, too cold under the thin comforter. In a dream, she wakes in her bedroom at home and sees falling snow. It feels like late afternoon. She wanders to the kitchen in her fleece nightie and Rich comes through the door dragging an enormous, bloodied caribou. He heaves this caribou into the centre of the room, then goes back outside and hauls in another. The kitchen fills with warm caribou carcasses until the mound reaches the ceiling, and then Rich tells her to start cutting—they are going to make caribou soup.

Yula wakes early and pictures Rich at the kitchen table: on his plate the same three boiled eggs and half-pound of bacon he eats every morning. She thinks about calling him, but of course he wouldn't answer—and what would she say to him? I miss you? They have never said that to each other. His presence in the house is like the birthmark on her right shoulder—so constant and unequivocal that she has never considered it outright.

Yula dresses in the same clothes she wore the day before. The sun has not yet risen and the town lies quiet. This quietness surprises her; she has never been to the desert before but imagined that, in the early hours when no one is about, it would make noise. That the earth would be alive as it is in the woods near her house, only in a different way. Instead of the swish of branches and the creak of tree trunks in the wind and the crows and starlings in the trees, the flat expanse of dirt would be somehow audible. Yula does not believe in God, nor would she ever go so far as to call herself a spiritual person. She does, however, believe that the land acts in ways that are not describable through science, nor through religion. That landscape possesses a kind of aliveness that sometimes shows itself, if you pay close enough attention. Not energies, exactly, because that sounds too mystical and new-agey. In the desert, she had imagined this aliveness would manifest itself in the ground. She would never try to explain this to someone, but if she did, she would liken it to an enormous, incredibly thin pancake, rising off the earth to meet the sky. A kind of connectedness between the land and the wide openness above. And the cacti, she imagined, the cacti would buzz like static.

Yula heard about the artist's residency nine months ago, from a travelling bat photographer. The night after she met the photographer, she lay in bed, Rich snoring next door and the house creaking in the wind, and fantasized about the aliveness of the desert. She fantasized about it for the next week, while she folded laundry at the Laundrolounge, and helped Rich butcher and freeze a buck and three rabbits, and met with the Ladies Group after work where the other women complained about menopause and their fat husbands. She imagined herself cross-legged in the desert—though in reality she hadn't been able to sit like that since her thirties—a sketchbook and pencil in hand, drawing cacti and the long flat sky and tumbleweeds that ambled by. In her fantasy, the landscape spoke through her. She had read this could happen—that a residency was the best way to open your creative spirit. She imagined she would feel awakened by the land, and her muse would sing.

At the end of that week, Yula sent a letter to the organizer of the residency, Wince Carver. She photocopied her three best sketches—Rich's workboot on the kitchen linoleum; three potatoes in a pot on the stove; the portrait of her mother on the wall above the bathtub—and sent them to him, along with an artist's statement and a photograph. She read somewhere that it wasn't a true artist's statement unless you hyperbolized, and so she stretched the boundaries of reality: increased her three months of drawing experience to four years—plus the thirteen or so she spent doodling as a child—and scribbled something about private showings of her work at several local galleries. She once visited a local gallery with the Ladies Group, and partook in a macramé tutorial, so it wasn't completely untrue. The instructor praised her plant hanger and suspended it in the gallery's front window. Yula had read, too, that many of the best artists were self-taught, and so she stressed in her application that she had *never* been to art school, not once.

She debated long about which photo of herself to send, and decided at last on one that Clay took on their twelfth wedding anniversary, when they carried a picnic up to the meadow and lay in the grass and drank cheap champagne, until they got into a fight over something trivial—she couldn't remember now what it was—and Clay stuffed all the food back in the picnic basket and hiked down without her. She hadn't wanted him to take the photo—this was before the fight—and put up a hand too late to stop him, so that in the photo her face was half-turned from the camera, hand mid-air like a conductor, a strand of hair picked up by the wind and blown across her neck. Her fingers were spread, cheek covered by her palm, but her eye was visible between index and middle fingers, mouth half-open below her pinky. She liked this photo, even though it showed her crooked incisor and widow's peak, because the light made her skin look warm and inviting; her windblown hair could almost be the hair of a carefree artist, in love with herself and with the world, sure of her talent and the future she would create for herself. The photograph was a good decade-and-a-half old, but the only recent photograph she could find was the one Rich insisted on taking of her at the Fall Fair, the year they went with the Kemps and their sadistic twin grandsons. In that photo, she sat on a prize-winning pony—a white, walleyed thing—and you could almost see it strain under her weight; its legs splayed, upper lip curled back. Yula's turtleneck—always that same cursed lavender turtleneck—was visibly tucked up in the underwire of her bra, her stomach exposed, flabs of skin shining in the sun like undercooked chicken. After Rich took the photo, Yula bought him a bag of candy corn, and the candy-corn man said to her, Your man's lucky to have a fine lady like you, with enough meat on her bones to keep him warm through the winter!

The motel, from the outside, resembles a barracks of sorts. It's the kind of place Yula imagines would house men with big, rough hands and scars on their faces; scars that—were you to ask them—the men would say they had had for so long, their origins had been forgotten. The men would wear tight, stiff denim and their vests would be lined with sheepskin, matted and yellowed from decades in the desert. The men came here to work the land; although the nature of their job was somewhat unclear, it was known to involve pickaxes and camaraderie and sweating, and required minds that would not break under the bitter desert sun. Yula imagines these men emerging from the eight doors of the motel in the virgin hours of morning—two from each room—the moon still protruding from the sky like a dime from a vending machine. The doors, like the rest of the motel, are a cold white; a desert rose painted on each by hand. The men would step from these doors in near unison and close them with care, not making a sound. Yula pictures their hands on the worn metal doorknobs—broad, callused palms and thick fingers, hair on their knuckles—turning in unison. Before they climbed up into their dented Ford trucks, the men would wipe their hands on the seats of their jeans and kick their boots against the tires. Then, two to a cab, they would drive off into the black desert.

Outside the motel, before daybreak, there are no men in thick denim. In the parking lot sit several trucks, a minivan, and a hatchback with a duct-taped window. Plastered on the gas station across the street are advertisements for Doritos and

Lotto tickets and microwaveable chicken wings. At Yula's feet lie cigarette butts and a rat's nest of blond hair and a flyer for Pig N' Pancake. Powerlines stretch overhead, black cables stark against a landscape of dust. On the outskirts of town stands a factory or mill of some sort, surrounded by a chain-link fence, its rusted white cylinders like hideous, bulging maggots. This desert is not the desert of Yula's imagination. She sees no cacti blooming pink and yellow, no sand, and the land does not feel alive—in fact it feels dry and dead. It's quiet out here, but not the quiet she imagined; a truck idles down the street and a porch door slams shut, an old Volvo drives by with the windows down and the news channel playing.

With her sketchbook and pencil case, Yula walks out along the still-dark road. She passes a woman who smokes on her porch, body draped in a beige men's button-down. The woman gestures at Yula with her head, a sort of reverse nod, the kind of motion the old timers back home make at Rich when they go into town. Yula smiles at the porch woman and the woman does not smile back. The windows of the trailers along the road are mostly dark, though she passes a few lit with blue light that illuminates the bags under the eyes of their inhabitants, glazed expressions fixed on *Jeopardy!* or infomercials. She walks until the buildings end, and the highway goes on through more dirt and small, spiky bushes and cacti. Among these plants and dirt are candy-bar wrappers and slushie cups and receipts and more cigarette butts. The dirt beneath her feet is not golden or red and does not crunch satisfyingly when she walks. Instead it is brown, but in a colourless, washed-out sort of way, and grinds under her Keds like walking on coarse salt.

The sun rises and Yula walks. The buildings drop behind her until she sees nothing but the long, flat road and the mountains in the distance. Already it is hot. Wary of scorpions and tarantulas and rattlesnakes, she keeps to the highway. Eventually she stops and sits on the tarmac. She looks at the dirt that stretches out in every direction; the mountains still so far in the distance, hazy and two-dimensional and the same washed-out colour as the ground. She closes her eyes and listens and hears only silence. She opens her eyes and lets them travel along the horizon, lets them rest on its edges until they begin to prickle and she has to blink. But the earth does not feel alive. Maybe, she decides, the way this landscape speaks is not audible.

But what is there to draw out here? Yula rests her sketchbook on her bent legs—already her body feels sore from the pavement—and contemplates the blank page. She is a landscape artist, a still-life artist, a figure drawer. A versatile artist. But she is not someone who draws from memory, nor from imagination. She begins to sketch the landscape, but its lines are flat and unvaried—the gradual arc of the mountains, an empty sky, scrags of desert flora. This landscape doesn't begin or end anywhere; it possesses neither parameters nor depth. All it is is dust. By the time she finishes her first landscape, the sun has become so hot that Yula has to squint to dull the glare of the white page. She begins a second drawing—this one of her sneakers on the road—but sweat drips into her eyes and onto her paper. Her damp fingers slide on her pencil and the lines come out all crooked. Her bones feel like they will crumble and adhere to the pavement, and so she hauls herself up from the highway and, eyes pressed to little slits, sleeves pushed up to the elbows and her turtleneck damp and sticking between her breasts and under her armpits, she trudges her sloppy, sagging body back to Angel City.

Later that afternoon, Doreen at the front desk tells Yula there must be a mistake—meals are not included in the residency. Wince Carver has yet to materialize and, never having been given a phone number to reach him, Yula has no way to contact him. She walks to the corner store and buys bologna and hotdog buns and mayonnaise and eats her dinner in the shade of a small bronze cow. The cow wears a medal around its neck that says "Wanda-Mae" and "Champion Sow." Yula washes her dinner down with warm Pepsi and then returns to her motel room and lies on the bed and stares at the ceiling. She considers calling Rich but doesn't. She pulls the Bible from the bedside table and flips through it. She begins to sketch the small square of parking lot visible through her window but gives up because there is nothing there to draw, only concrete and cigarette butts. There is no TV in her room. She walks to the closet and opens it and inside are three cigarette butts and two crumpled-up receipts from Lou Harvey's. Yula hangs her few clothing items. She climbs under the covers of her bed and listens to the fan going, until she falls asleep and dreams that she is a small cow, roaming the desert with a mouthful of pencils.

For the next several days, Yula attempts various methods to awaken her creative spirit. She rises in complete darkness and walks along the highway, this time in the opposite direction, takes with her sunglasses and a bottle of water and a pillow to sit on. She stays out there for hours and fills page after page of her sketchbook with the endless line of the horizon, until a trucker drives by and offers her a ride back to town. She draws various buildings in Angel City, though the town's inhabitants don't take kindly to this, and when she tries to explain that she is an artist, that she is completing a residency here and have they heard of it, they give her suspicious looks and spit in the dirt and wipe their mouths on the backs of their hands. Sometimes they leave her alone and other times they tell her to get lost. She visits the Catholic church, the corner store, Lou Harvey's diner, and the hardware store, which sells guns and duct tape and fireworks and flypaper and pepperoni. She asks people if she can sketch their portraits, but they adamantly oppose her advances—with the exception of Father Parker, an obese forty-year-old priest with long black hair, who relents on the condition that she attend mass on Sunday. For two entire days, she starves herself in her hotel room, blinds closed, and does not venture out once, having read somewhere that many artists produce their best work in complete isolation and deprivation. She draws the bed, the table, the framed cowboy above the toilet, her toothbrush, the cigarette butts in the closet, the little bits of her fingernails she chews up and spits into the sink. She sits in the bathtub for three hours and produces nineteen drawings of her feet, but always they come out like the limbs of an ogre, toes thick and stubby, toenails jagged. She runs out of things to sketch in her room and tries to masturbate—hopes maybe this will bring inspiration—but all she can think about is the unending flatness of the desert. After an hour of frustration, she orgasms, then falls asleep on her bed with her fingers in her mouth.

—

By the eighth day, or maybe it's the ninth, Wince Carver has not shown. Yula thinks about calling Rich but doesn't want him to know that maybe he was right about the residency. Maybe it is all a big joke, after all. Her sleep patterns worsen, and she dreams that she wanders the desert for the rest of her life, manically sketching one identical desert plant after the other, until all she can see are zigzags. She begins to sleep during the day and venture out at night, to avoid both the sun and the townspeople. She walks along the highway for hours, sits and draws the shadows. The nights are clear and the moonlight makes the now-familiar landscape tamer, somehow, and more approachable. The ground remains dusty and dry and dead, but there are bats in the air, and sometimes coyotes in the distance.

Rarely do cars pass by at night, but once a motorcycle's head-light appears in the distance, and a man drives up and slows and stops. He wears black leather pants with tassels down the leg, and a leather jacket, and boots with metal plates over the toes. His helmet is bright orange with a white suede strap—the kind of helmet Carla from the Ladies Group wears when she rides to her secretary job on her lemon-yellow scooter. The man wears cheap sports sunglasses, too small for his head, and he takes these off and his eyes sit tiny and sunken in an otherwise handsome face. His skin looks so smooth that it both unsettles and excites Yula. She feels no fear toward this man, alone with him in the moonlit desert. He looks down at her, where she sits on her motel pillow, legs stretched straight out on the tarmac. She thinks she must look like a child. She feels like a child.

Hey, did you hurt yourself? the man asks, and his voice comes out several tones higher than Yula expects it to.

I'm just drawing, Yula says, though the paper in her hands is blank and she has been staring out at the horizon for an amount of time that feels infinite.

Yeah? he says. What do you call this one? White night in the desert?

Yula closes her sketchbook. The man laughs a kind laugh.

You that artist-lady Doreen keeps telling me about? The one in room six? She says you're wacko, crazy-involved in the "creative process." He does air quotes with his fingers but does not appear to be mocking her.

Are you Ribs? asks Yula. The man is younger than Doreen by a good ten or fifteen years, his demeanour comforting in a way that she would never associate with the front-desk woman.

Ah, she told you about me, did she? The man grins and his teeth shine small and sharp, like a rat terrier's. She's quite the girl, he says. I know she comes across as a little standoffish, but she's a sweetheart. You know, I should get you to draw a portrait of her for me. I'd pay ya. Doreen's a little shy but I betcha I could convince her.

Yula can't imagine Doreen would consent to such a thing, but she smiles and says yes, of course she could do that. Then adds, I've done lots of commissioned portraits back home. She trips over this word *commissioned*, but Ribs doesn't seem to notice.

How about tomorrow? Does that sound good? He offers her a ride back to town on his motorcycle, but she tells him she likes the walk—and it's true.

The next morning Yula sleeps until noon, then walks to Lou Harvey's and eats scrambled eggs and hash browns and drinks two cans of PBR for courage and inspiration. She meets Ribs outside the motel at two. He wears his leather motorcycle pants, and a bright green button-down with the sleeves rolled up, and a bolo tie. He carries a black JanSport backpack and a thick, rolled-up sheet of white paper. In the daylight, his face still has the same striking softness to it, and without his helmet Yula sees that he is bald. His scalp glistens in the desert sun like the dome of the observatory back home, and his sun-glasses hang from his shirt pocket. Ribs hugs Yula, and her face presses into his chest. He smells like cloves and ChapStick.

Doreen is real excited for this, Ribs says. Bits of green peek from the cracks between his teeth. He hands Yula the rolled-up sheet. I brought you this to draw on, he says. It's old wallpaper but it should work, right?

Doreen emerges from the lobby. She wears a purple west-ern shirt, tucked into high-waisted jeans with rhinestones on the pockets. Two tight braids hang down past her shoulders—hair pulled back with such ferocity that it gives her eyebrows a surprised quality.

Hey baby, says Ribs, and puts an arm around her. Doreen looks at Yula with supreme boredom.

Can we walk to your house from here? asks Yula, unsure at whom to direct the question, since it's unclear to her where either Doreen or Ribs resides.

Oh, says Ribs. Our house is kinda in a state of construction right now. I was thinking we could do it in your room. In your artistic suite. Your studio. That way you can really feel free to let your art flow. He flashes her the same big grin he gave her out on the moonlit highway.

—

In the motel room, Ribs takes charge of setting the scene for the portrait. Yula feels relief at this but acts as though she is doing Ribs a big favour by handing over so much artistic responsibility. Ribs moves like an energetic child: pushes furniture to the wall and moves the bed so it sits under the window. He begins to sweat and unbuttons his shirt down to his bellybutton. I'm thinking it'll be a full-body portrait, he says, and Yula gives him a serious nod.

Doreen sits down on the bed and lights a cigarette, smokes and taps the ash onto the bedspread. Yula excuses herself to go the bathroom, and when she re-emerges Doreen has taken off her shirt. Underneath, her breasts are bare, and they spill down her front, nipples huge and brown. A wooden rosary hangs in her cleavage and there is a horse's head tattooed on her left breast, its face stretched and misshapen. Yula hides her surprise at Doreen's nudity, and acts as though she is accustomed to drawing half-naked women. Ribs pulls the small table and folding chair into the centre of the room and Yula sits and unrolls the sheet of wallpaper. It covers the table and hangs over the sides. Doreen looks sullen and emotionless, but she arranges herself on the bed and holds still. She faces Yula straight on, back against the wall and long legs spread wide, feet flat on the floor. On any other woman, this might be a sexual pose, but Doreen looks more like an old rancher or a football coach than a *Playboy* model. She plants her hands on her thick thighs, elbows bent, and the cigarette hangs from her lips. A bit of ash falls onto her breast and she lets it stay there. She does not remove her glasses and her big eyes look at Yula with indifference.

Yula had thought Ribs would leave the room while she completed the portrait, but instead he stays. At first he paces with excitement, then apologizes and pulls the armchair up next to the table and sits. Yula can feel his hyperactive energy and he bounces his legs up and down; his shirt hangs open and she can't help but glance at his pale chest, his tiny nipples, his torso scrawny and hairless. Terrified that Ribs will realize her incompetency and inexperience, Yula begins to sketch Doreen. She starts with the eyes, but one ends up higher than the other, and the glasses come out wrong. She draws the chin too low and the forehead too wide, the neck much too long. Ribs doesn't seem to care. He watches her draw in fascination, and compliments her work. It takes Yula an hour to draw Doreen's face. Ribs brings her a glass of water. She draws Doreen's arms and waist, too scared to attempt her expansive breasts and tattoo, leaving them to fill in later. She takes a break and Ribs goes out and brings back fried chicken. Doreen doesn't move from the bed, but when Ribs brings the chicken he kneels in front of her and she leans forward and kisses him with tongue. Yula knows she uses tongue because she can hear it. After the chicken, Ribs brings Doreen a face cloth from the bathroom and she wipes her mouth and fingers on it, and while she does this Ribs plays with her nipples in a distracted way.

Yula continues to draw and she fills in Doreen's breasts and then spends another hour on the horse tattoo, which comes out bad but not worse than the real thing. Doreen's head sits too low on the page and so Yula shortens the torso, terrified that she will run out of room. She attempts to draw Doreen's thighs, but lacks experience with foreshortening. She erases and redraws them five times, and still they look like tree trunks, though Ribs doesn't seem concerned, and Doreen sits, disinterested. Ribs smokes a cigarette and sings "Cotton Eye Joe" and clicks the heels of his boots together. They take another break and Ribs brings them Hickory Sticks and cold Coronas, and Yula and Ribs sit at the table together while Doreen naps, sitting up on the bed. It gets dark outside and Ribs leaves again and comes back with a light on a long pole. He stands this next to the bed and points it on Doreen, who wakes up and lights a cigarette. Yula looks at her paper and wonders how she will fit Doreen's knees and calves and feet into the small space that remains at the bottom.

Ribs says, I can't wait to frame this. He says, Yula, this has been great. Doreen and I are so grateful to get to work with an artist like you. What an experience. His grin is perpetual and it's a genuine grin, Yula can tell.

Yula says, Aren't you getting tired, Doreen? Do you want to finish tomorrow?

Doreen doesn't answer but Ribs says, Do *you* need to take a break, Yula? Why don't you take a break. Doreen and I don't have anywhere to be.

Yula says that okay, she might go stretch her legs for a minute. She puts on her turtleneck and walks down to Lou Harvey's and looks in the windows and watches the regulars eat their steaks. She stretches her stiff neck and massages her butt. She walks back to the motel and Ribs is in the bathroom washing his hands, Doreen still on the bed where she has been since early afternoon. Ribs comes out of the bathroom with his belt buckle undone and he leaves it undone and he says, Good walk?

Yula sits down at the table but her hand shakes from holding a pencil for so long. Yula, says Ribs, take all the time you need. We're not in a hurry, he says. Why don't you rest a little longer.

Some part of Yula wishes Doreen and Ribs will leave so she can sleep, but another part of her, the bigger part that is bossy and accustomed to winning, reminds her that art is pain; that this residency is the start of her serious career as an artist; that she will never make it if she can't persevere through a little exhaustion.

Yula, says Ribs, and looks at her with such a sympathetic and pained expression that she would do almost anything not to see him disappointed. Yula, he says. Take a break. It's okay.

Yula puts down her pencil and Ribs says, Why don't you go sit on the bed with Doreen? He smiles at Yula. Doreen is smoking again. Ribs says, Go sit with her on the bed, you deserve a rest. You both do.

Yula stands and moves toward Doreen, simultaneously drawn to and repulsed by the half-nude woman on her bed, the wide eye of the horse on her breast staring at Yula. Doreen neither smiles nor glares at her, as if anything that has or will ever happen in Doreen's life is just part of a routine. She snuffs her cigarette out on the bedframe, pulls her feet up onto the bed—her first change in position since her arrival in the motel room—and holds her knees with her hands, legs still spread wide.

Go on, says Ribs. You can sit in her lap, it's okay.

Yula will later wonder why she felt no emotion, one way or another, at the whole experience. But in the moment, she sees no reason not to sit in Doreen's lap; sees no reason why she, too, should not be unconcerned and unemotional, why she should not both make Ribs happy and give in to her own fatigue, even if it means sitting between the legs of this half-nude woman. And so she scoots her butt up on the bed, between Doreen's large thighs, and Doreen puts her arms around Yula. Doreen is a good five inches taller, and her floppy breasts envelop Yula in a way that, Yula realizes, is not unwelcome. She tries, and fails, to remember the last time someone held her like this. She leans her head back against Doreen's breasts and closes her eyes and they stay this way for a long time. Doreen's breath becomes deep and even and Yula lets her own eyes close, lets herself fall back into a soft slumber. She dreams, for the first time, that she walks in a desert that is fully alive—more alive, even, than in her fantasies. She hears the buzzing of cacti and sees the dirt vibrate; sees the sky and land meet and adhere to one another; sees this all under a sun that, rather than wash out the land to a flat brown, gives her surroundings depth and substance. She dreams that she sits on the side of the road and draws landscape after landscape that flows from her hand.

Later—because what happens seems to happen of its own accord, and no one is invested or bothered, one way or another—Yula takes her shirt off and Doreen touches Yula's breasts and they kiss, just a little, Doreen pushing her tongue into Yula's mouth, expression unchanged. And Yula sucks on Doreen's nipples, although neither of them removes their pants and Ribs doesn't take his off either, though he sits and grins in a way that suggests nothing surprises him and he is as happy here as anywhere else. At one point Ribs pulls an old Polaroid camera out of his JanSport and takes two photographs of the women: one of Yula sitting shirtless in Doreen's lap, Doreen looking at the camera and Yula looking out the window; and another of Yula with her head in Doreen's lap, Doreen's breasts hanging over her with one nipple in Yula's mouth, while Doreen smokes a cigarette. Afterwards, Yula puts her shirt on and finishes the portrait, and her hand does not shake, and Doreen's legs come out too short and her feet get cut off and the drawing looks nothing like her, but Ribs says, It's a masterpiece. And Ribs gives Yula the Polaroid of her in Doreen's lap, plus a hundred-and-seventy-five dollars, and finally Doreen stands and puts her shirt back on. When they leave, Doreen doesn't say goodbye, but Ribs gives Yula a hug. By this time it is early morning and Yula lies in her bed, and her sleep is so deep that she dreams of nothing.

The next day, Yula says hi to Doreen, and Doreen says hi back and doesn't smile, and Yula doesn't ask about Wince Carver. She continues to go out into the desert, mostly at night, and still the land feels dead, though this no longer surprises her. Her drawings come out flat and lifeless, but she no longer anticipates a time when this will change. If to become of-the-desert is not to become one with its washed-out dryness, but rather to realize that there is nothing here, and to accept this without emotion, then maybe this is what Yula becomes, if only for a short month. She doesn't see Ribs again, except once when she spots him and Doreen through the window at Lou Harvey's, eating steak. Doreen doesn't smile but she picks a piece of steak off Ribs's plate with her fork and feeds it to him and he laughs and then they kiss.

Yula goes to Father Parker's sermon and draws the stained-glass windows and the painting of Jesus on the cross. She draws the factory at the edge of town and the broken furniture in the yards and the silhouettes of coyotes in the desert at night. She draws a car that crashes into a telephone pole one morning, and the poutine spilled onto the pavement, upon collision, by the drunk driver. She draws and draws and though her drawings are perhaps still no good, they become a reflex—the most obvious thing to do. And at the end of the month she packs all her clothes and five sketchbooks back in her little suitcase, and hands Doreen her room keys, who doesn't smile but says, Seeya around. And Yula gets in a taxi, and she sits in the back as they drive out of Angel City, and she sleeps the whole way to the airport. She boards a plane just before sunset, a Polaroid tucked somewhere at the bottom of her suitcase. And when she lands in Canada, Rich picks her up from the airport, a warm, dead buck in the back of his pickup, its head lolling over the tailgate. She considers telling Rich that she missed him, but instead she stares out the passenger-side window as they drive out of town and traces the jagged mountains with her finger.

CANISIA LUBRIN

NO ID OR WE COULD BE BROTHERS

After his usual taxi rounds, Gregory was supposed to pick us up from that restaurant on King Street. I saw him arrive at the corner, and by the brief flash of his blue sedan's reverse lights on the street-side I knew he had decided to park, and I turned back to Andi, who nodded, so we raised our glasses to finish off our beers. Gregory had known where Andi and I would be waiting. And even though this wasn't the first time he had told us to wait someplace and did not show up exactly, there we were, Andi and I, unbothered by the twenty minutes that had passed between seeing Gregory's car park and the argument we were now having about Sara. We were used to being consumers of misery. We were unsurprised by those who would manufacture any of it. The last time Gregory'd kept us waiting, in the Distillery District, we were arguing about some grand-sounding-but-empty thing we'd read about feminism and badness in the national paper. And we'd eaten tapas and drank liquors and lost track of waiting. The most effortless expenditure of our time, all the grooming we'd need accomplished before we were to meet our lovers that night. So, by the time we no longer cared that Gregory had stood us up yet again, we simply took another taxi and said nothing much to each other the whole ride to Sara's house.

Last night on King Street, I think, I saw him step out of that car, just briefly, peripherally. His driver's door swung out like some madness lived in its hinges. I wish now that I had decided to leave Andi and our argument at the table to walk a few paces toward him. I should have hailed him out and asked after the mad swinging of his door. Anyone who knew Gregory knew how much he treated anyone swinging open or hard-shutting his car doors like a lamentation. I now wish that even if he may not have heard me as he got back into his driver's seat, carefully closing the door, he might have sensed some uncannily familiar presence as he drove off. I might have seen Gregory laughing in his rear-view mirror. I might have seen someone in the passenger seat whose shape I likely could not make out no matter the effort I would put into this seeing. And as the car moved into traffic, I might have had a thing to say about this person's polished, heavily ringed hand flying backward and forward, and I might have seen a few things more as they went out of sight.

All of this somehow made it into the police report.

Gregory, an intense man, those who knew him might say, had been pressed into rigidity by the half-forgotten landscape of his older life. He had left his family on some island waiting as he accumulated, in the arteries of the metropolis, many things worth numbers less than zero. He had come from what most people viewed as nothing. The tough plantation life, now only memory, of a now mythic Caribbean. He would often say Sara was the most human part of his life and he longed for her warmth well before he could clock out at all odd hours. But leave me to the small rooms of my relinquishing. We are so much alike, Gregory and I. We even look alike. We could be brothers, though most of what we are is that we love the same woman. And now he's as remote and distant from my present as a forgotten age when gold coins passed for legal tender.

Before the restaurant on King Street that night, Andi and I shared a whisky at my place and then called Gregory to make plans for after his shift. The driver who picked us up to take us to the restaurant wore blistered lips, still smiling like a thing too familiar with cold, cold air.

"King Street," Andi said, texting wildly on her phone. The driver just nodded, turned the volume way up on Coltrane's "Venus," and drove off.

"Anywhere you say," Gregory would have answered. But we hadn't seen Gregory since last weekend at Sara's house—not at Gregory's, the half-legal refugee who couldn't afford lodging on his own terms—and Andi made a joke about the blessing of Coltrane's obnoxious sax giving us a chance to plan how we would bring up Sara's newest failed pregnancy to Gregory and why I would do the job if Gregory couldn't. We could be ignorant, apathetic motherfuckers sometimes, but this wasn't one of those times. I would do things for Gregory that I would do for nobody else. I'd have a child I did not want if that would help mend the ravages of what he believed was his failed manhood. Even if I knew he could not be convinced to accept any such help from me, I was willing to invent that future.

We left that first restaurant nearing eleven and decided to walk a few blocks south through the half-heavy air of the city. We decided we might as well hit up that after-hours underground restaurant for tropical cocktails, the downtown's best-kept secret, owned by two gay Bajan fellas. I called Gregory's cell, just in case, to let him know we'd decided to change locations. There was no answer so we took another cab. Some kilometres down the road, at the corner of Adelaide and Spadina, a young man dressed like a *Vogue* model in black high threads and white Doc Martens, a leather satchel clutched under his right arm, stood dangerously close to the live traffic lane our driver pulled into indiscriminately and stopped in. The driver flung a small brown package out the front passenger window, and it landed at the feet of the young man. The driver then gave a quick glance in his rear-view mirror as though to confirm that we had registered what just happened and that we knew it was none of our business. He had that air of a neighbour who spells his rank to all the rest by never locking his doors no matter the time of day or night. You knew to just let a man like that be.

"You two got a sense of adventure, don't you?" the driver said as he merged back into traffic without so much as a lilt of concern in his voice.

"We may have too many," Andi answered.

"If it doesn't break our hearts, we don't want it," I added.

The driver nodded and lowered the volume on the car stereo.

He asked, "Not to change the subject without warning, but did you folks hear of what happened?"

"What happened?" Andi asked.

"Taxi man from south. Some hooligan cops did him severe. He's at St. Joseph's hospital fighting for any damn life right now. They say he hadn't got no ID on him. At the time of the altercation, they say he was off-duty. His roof light was off."

"From south?" I asked.

"Southside. Jamestown. But what fucks me up is how these hooligans who did him nasty carry ID badges that turn every plain thing in their hands into a weapon."

"Which taxi man? What's his name?" Andi asked, impatience cracking her breath.

"I think he's from Antigua or Tortola or some such place."

Andi and I looked at each other. We could both taste the heaviness of Gregory's absence in the air. The uncharacteristic laughing that had raised our brows that last time we saw him closed in on us as the driver kept on with his litany of judicial objections.

Andi dialed Sara's cell and it rang out. She tried Sara's house line and it rang out. She tried her work line and left a frantic voicemail, finally. The driver, it seemed, could not be bothered to be sobered by our unquiet. "Anyway. They say those cops who took him down like, you know, one of those things you watch on *Planet Earth* documentaries. Wild cat versus tame cat. They wrote in their police report 'immigrant,' and you two know they mean every syllable of that accusation. We cab drivers, we like a brotherhood. We talk, man, we talk. We keep no secrets."

"Yes. Yes. I see," I said, cajoling calm out of some imaginary place. I closed my eyes. I took a deep breath. I thought I understood nothing exceptionally true.

"What did you do before you started driving people?" Andi asked the driver. I'm sure she was desperate to change the subject because she sensed my panic. She has always been better at coping than I.

"Two degrees in political science have done me no good here or there," the driver said. "Anyway. You take a decent man. I know him, you see? I know that taxi man," the driver said. "A decent man, but whatever you think he is, you give him one more reason to think of life as indifferent education, right?"

"I see," I said again.

"Don't you want to know how I know?" the driver added, his voice cool, recondite.

"What do you think you know?" I asked.

"Look. Listen close. Some woman called the police about a taxi driver who was harassing her over an underpaid fare. She claims he started pressing buttons all over the machine when she wouldn't entertain his hand on her thigh."

"Listen," Andi said. "Can you take us elsewhere?"

The driver nodded and Andi told him our new destination. I was thirsty. All I was was thirsty.

The driver rounded the corner near Lincoln Avenue as the now-rising sun rusted the view. I threw some bills at him and stumbled out of the back, slamming the door. At six-fifty in the morning, I called Gregory's phone. It rang all the way to voicemail. And again every few minutes, each time until the ringing stopped and the voicemail clicked on. I went to the police station instead of St. Joseph's, where Andi went. I've been known to abandon sense before. I stood in their lobby, dry-mouthed, for a long while before someone paid me any mind. Andi was supposed to call me the minute she got into Sara's apartment to check if she was there before going to the hospital. She would seduce the doorman like she had done many times before, and he would let her in. She hadn't called in the hour it took me to finally speak to one of the cops.

"Discharged," the officer said.

"Discharged?" I wanted to be sure I had heard her correctly.

"You want to know what happened to your friend, you say?"

"I do," I said.

"Then I already told you you should go to the hospital because it will be a while before he is discharged. I can't tell you anything about what's under investigation."

"What's his name?"

"You've given me a description of the suspect, and all I've said is I cannot tell you what's under investigation."

"Why is he a suspect?" I asked again, fearing I hadn't been clear the first time. I should have known better than to expect more.

"Look, sit down. I'm not working this case. There's nothing I can add. So I suspect you will be better off where your friend is."

I walked out into the coldest of Octobers. Breath as good as knives in the throat. At St. Joseph's hospital I could barely recognize this man who looks like me. Gregory was hooked up to all manner of tube and machine. And I wondered if this was the fate of every human body, if this was one way of a hope that hardly matters, every human body broken into, demanding an evolution into machine, dismissive of every felt sense.

Andi and Sara were there in that hallway peering into the ICU. Sara's body couldn't still itself. She was never particularly good at stillness. I walked up next to her and held her. She did not hold me back, but she leaned toward Andi as a child would lean into her parent's grasp. I wished that Gregory would look up and I would make new meaning from the way his eyes are barely visible through the swollen tissue around them. He would have protested seeing my attempt at carrying his woman and I would have let her go. We would have given all of our attention to one another; he would have sat up, detached himself from the machines, and walked out of the ICU a new man.

"What happened, Sara? Do you know anything?" I asked.

"I was waiting for G for thirty minutes or so," Sara began. "He was supposed to drop me off at home before he came for you two on King Street. I was impatient and in a hurry to get home so I was on the lookout for him. I sat in that hard plastic chair looking out through the window and thought two taxis that pulled up at separate times were G when they were not. Someone must have called the cops at some point. Somewhere between that realization and my anger and looking down to read an article on my phone, sirens began to wail about some-one in danger and I looked up and saw them damn flashing lights already on the street-side. I can't tell you how much time had passed. Of course I went out. Of course I was screaming for the cops to stop hitting before I saw who it was they were laying low. They were making noise about resisting arrest and just laying G low like some game. In these moments, you know, you want things to add up that don't add up."

MICHAEL LAPOINTE

CANDIDATE

Spencer showed me the margins. The symbol cartwheeled down the page. We'd seen it in a movie. The bad guys wore the symbol on their arms. Spencer was the only other boy who'd seen the movie, so we could laugh about it together.

At my desk, I tried drawing the symbol, but the pencil sometimes went the other way. For a while, I forgot how it was meant to go. Then I thought about the guys in the movie, and it came.

I laughed and looked to Spencer. His head was down, pencil working on the page. I made one symbol after another. Every time it worked, it was exciting.

I wondered what else Spencer was drawing. What else had he seen?

The teacher stood up. Spencer's head stayed down. Now she came up the aisle. In the movie, we'd seen what happened to the bad guys. I rubbed out my symbols and brushed the dust away.

The teacher asked for Spencer's paper, but I guess he'd erased his symbols, or maybe it wasn't so bad after all. She just handed back the page and told us to keep working.

Spencer and I tolerated other shows but only really liked *The Simpsons*. *The Simpsons* taught us the culture. For years, we'd see something in a movie or on TV and finally understand the reference from *The Simpsons*. When we encountered the actual source, we already knew how to make it funny. The only other thing we watched was a tape of Spencer's sister getting thrown from a horse.

Everything Spencer said was funny. He talked like *The Simpsons*. You didn't have to know why.

One time, he said, "Ask me if I'm a tree."

"Are you a tree?"

"No."

That was the funniest thing we'd ever heard.

"You thought we were joking with this campaign," I remind the woman from the CBC. "But Dom is reaching people outside the bubble. If I were trying to reassure a certain bloc, I might point to his charitable donations. Go ask SickKids about Dom Crossman. But we aren't motivated by reassuring moderates. There are people who don't pick up when you people call. There's a country out there, unlike the one you carry around in notebooks. Dom's for them, all the way. At this point, he can't be denied the nomination. I think the party knows that."

A few months into our campaign for the nomination, reporters started interviewing Wei and me, "the millennial brain trust of Dom Crossman's candidacy"—a label that annoys Wei, who's forty. They started asking how a retired hockey coach could work his way into federal politics, apparently not realizing their questions drew him further in.

I give credit where it's due: Wei polishes the Dom Crossman product—broad shoulders, double Windsor knot, white side-burns shading into black. She strictly limits his vocabulary, runs the lint roller down his breast; she makes him viable to the casual eye gliding over a TV screen.

My role is different. Reporters call me a strategist, but it's not like I'm hunched in some tent, moving armies on a map. To an outsider, my day-to-day would appear laughable: I scrutinize memes; I dragnet comments; I absorb varieties of anger. Where others hear nothing, I detect a mood. And when I finally speak, people lean in to hear me. The results of what I say aren't quantifiable, except, of course, we're here at the convention and no one wants to talk about a candidate unless his name is Dom Crossman.

People thought Spencer was Trench Coat Mafia. It wasn't a hard category to fall into. All you had to do was point a french fry at somebody. Call the principal's office and breathe heavy—everyone got the day off. But Spencer really did fit the profile, pale and stubby and delaying his first shave. He had this weird flair for slobbiness. He'd wear one collared shirt on top of another; he'd stalk the hallways in fingerless black gloves and supermarket shades. Everyone knew he played *Counter-Strike* at an elite level.

Spencer was my best friend, but we weren't treated with the same suspicion. I was taller, cleaner, able to pass into groups without projecting a suffocating air. I knew the names of the people around me.

Spencer and I were fascinated by Columbine, by anything fucked up. We downloaded scraps of video off Kazaa.

"Check out this fucked-up takeoff."

"Check out this fucked-up crackhead."

"Check out this execution."

On the Hewlett-Packard in Spencer's basement, I saw a Chechen rebel getting stabbed in the throat; I saw a man getting fucked by a horse. Child soldiers ran through a minefield in some distant civil war. Then we'd Alt-Tab back to *CS*, or turn our attention to TV, or take a break and defrost something to eat. When another video finished downloading, we watched it.

We liked the idea of being desensitized. It was something to be cultivated by subjecting yourself to constant imagery, like a game of who can hold a burning match the longest. We hoped our curiosity would lead us to a place out of reach; that was where we wanted to be. We could look at people and know we'd seen things that would disgust and horrify them.

That was the aura of the Trench Coat Mafia, but I knew Spencer, at least, wasn't a killer. The thing with so many of these massacres was that, in the end, the shooters killed themselves. It was real for them in a way it could never be for Spencer. He didn't want to die. Name something worth dying for.

Spencer said, "How do you kill a thousand flies?"

"How?"

"You hit an Ethiopian in the face with a frying pan."

Jokes had to be on the margins. We made jokes about Jews, jokes about blacks, jokes about women. Gay sex lurked behind all our innuendo. Being monstrous was the funny thing. It said more if you just made the other guy go *wow* than if you made him actually laugh.

Only we could handle the material. We performed at a very particular frequency. We'd never want to be overheard. Yet I always pictured a woman—white, respectable, like Spencer's sister—hearing our jokes, and she became the final object of ridicule. Her face contorted; she was afraid of laughing.

Spencer and I considered ourselves fluid. The final safeguard against monstrosity was that we didn't have a sense of self at all. In fact, we'd mastered what we'd been told was the basis for all morality: to put yourself in other people's shoes. So we could be bigots, wife-beaters, lovers one instant to the next—a shuffle of reference. If you thought we were serious, the joke was on you.

Wei worries about disgrace. She says it's the natural conclusion of most candidates with the volatile momentum of Dom Crossman. The great fear is of exploding just as you're taking flight. She's described a vision of Dom blowing it here at the convention. He could succumb to his confidence, as if the game were in hand, and start slaughtering some of our campaign's sacred cows: jobs, God, the intrinsic goodness of the people. All in an instant—evaporation. "You'll look for me"—and Wei pats me on the shoulder—"but I'll be gone."

Despite her genius, it's possible that even Wei doesn't realize the roll we're on. She might be just a little too last-generation. She still really feels every scandal.

And our campaign has weathered its share of them: tax discrepancies, plagiarized college papers, an off-script joke about Mental Health Awareness Month. But I encourage Dom to shoot from the hip. Sometimes I tell him: "We're pushing out from the centre." He internalizes that kind of strategy, force confronting force. I've been spoken of as a hazardous influence by members of his inner circle, and I understand. Their curse is that they have to worry about every last vulnerability.

I'm not like them. I accept that Dom is an imperfect vessel; it wouldn't surprise me if he had brain trauma from his playing days. I dream of a candidate who steps out of the margins already complete—fluid and faceless, a total negation.

The Ontario Teachers' Federation picketed in our first year of middle school. Spencer and I welcomed the strike, which dragged on for weeks. But we also became aware of our status, in the clash between the union and the government, as the lowest priority—chattel, basically—and this formed the first occasion of our taking political offence. We began to frame ourselves as marginal.

In our view, they were all morons—our teachers and our government—though the teachers were slightly worse because they complained directly to us. How many times had class been interrupted so the teacher could bemoan how there weren't enough supplies due to government cuts? It was laughable how small our teachers were willing to appear in their efforts to turn us against the government. Cuts, cuts, cuts— like the school was bleeding out from a billion wounds.

Politics now became a central topic for Spencer and me. Political knowledge was something you were expected to acquire when not around each other. When it came to news of the world, we liked stories of war and terrorism. It was adult to imagine what would happen if, for instance, Pakistan leaked a nuclear weapon, one you could fit in a briefcase, to religious fanatics. When it came to domestic issues, we took a general stance against welfare and taxation—people leeching off hard work. We pictured our teachers, who barely knew our names, always craving more.

At our high school, you could take comp sci. Spencer and I sat side by side in the computer lab and worked on all the projects together. I wasn't very good at programming, but Spencer covered for me. I think he was glad to have me as a partner; he could do the work alone. He coded a tank warfare game that hooked up between computers, so two players could go at it from across the lab. Despite a bunch of bugs, the game impressed everybody. Spencer called it *Napalm Sunburn*.

Comp sci ended up as one of my highest grades, and I took it as a natural fact that Spencer would design games for a living. But he wasn't even the best student in class. We kept an eye on a girl named Meera, who bused in from another district so she could attend a school with a computer lab. Meera never looked away from the screen; in her glasses, the blue light glowed. When we fell silent, I could hear her keyboard chattering. Spencer called Meera the Muskrat because of the wild eyebrows, the matted hair, the dark down on her cheeks.

Meera's projects were totally clean and actually useful. Spencer hated watching her presentations. She seemed aware of functions that adults needed performed and designed sharp, intuitive interfaces for just those purposes. Meanwhile, we couldn't imagine anything outside *Napalm Sunburn*.

The school organized an annual plant sale to supplement its budget, and our comp sci teacher gave Meera the special assignment of programming an online ordering system. Parents who used the system could get their plants a day early. This particular program was Meera's masterpiece. We did a beta test in class, and I remember feeling like her system somehow made the computer itself run faster, like a glass of water in a marathon.

The night the system went live, Spencer messaged me on MSN. He said the Muskrat had made a big mistake. There wasn't a character limit to the ordering fields, so you could submit unlimited amounts of data to the system. By the time I got to the site, Spencer was already copying hundreds of thousands of pages of text into the fields. He told me to help, and I did it for laughs. We forced reams of text down the throat of Meera's code. I'd never used a computer that way; it was a creative act—compulsive, unconscious. After a dozen submissions, the site was taking forever to load. In another minute, it was gone.

Monday morning was when parents who'd used Meera's system were supposed to collect their orders. The plants were kept in a small gated area against the side of the school. When I arrived that morning, the gate was locked. No one was around. Under the tarp, the plants were in shadow.

Our comp sci teacher gave a speech about hacking. Computers were a liberating force, he said—by which he meant a force for good. We could be the vanguard of all that, if we wanted. I looked over at Meera. Her computer was off; she was staring at her hands. Beside me, Spencer had already started on the next program.

—

At first, people saw the Dom Crossman campaign as obviously right, then possibly left, then hopefully centre, until finally it depended on where you stood. I tell Dom: track along the spectrum. I tell him: wait until they've found the face they're searching for.

Lately, I've observed a kind of delirium in our supporters. They actually dance at our rallies, swaying together and laughing.

The weekend of the convention has been building up to Dom's address. But when, in the first movement of the speech, he mentions border security, a woman unfolds a sign: WELCOME THE NEWCOMERS.

I can't hear what she's yelling. Some members of the party boo; others applaud. She's drowned out. I look over at Wei, who fretfully awaits the moment of disgrace. Is this it?

Everywhere we've gone, the Newcomers are the fixed idea. I don't have a strong feeling on the matter, but to the extent that they embody the borderless flow—of jobs, capital, culture—I advise Dom to maintain a stance of general antagonism. That comes naturally to him; he was a bruiser for the Leafs in the '80s.

"I boarded Hartford's top prospect," he once told me, plucking his eyebrows in a pocket mirror. "And he got this burst fracture in the spine. Put an end to his career, like that—fresh-faced youngster. And people called me all sorts of things, but my family never went hungry."

Vis-à-vis the Newcomers, we're only absorbing the spirit as we find it. "You'll do something about them," a woman told us at a rally. "I've got three families in my neighbourhood alone. Nobody's working. The women are pregnant. You can see them on the steps. Our local boys are scared to go by the building."

Dom said, "You'll feel safe in your own country, ma'am."

And he held her small hand. Her eyes beamed up at him with gladness.

Now he stands at the podium as the protestor is strong-armed off the convention floor. But Dom's in a magnanimous frame of mind. Wei can relax.

"It's good, it's good," he says. "This is democracy, folks, pure and simple. She has the right to yell. And we have the right to yell. Show her some courtesy on the way out, will you? Don't let her trip. I don't want anything happening to her."

From the edges of the room, at just the right moment, Wei strikes up a chant. Dom exhorts: "Strength! In! Numbers!"

I don't like the mob, but I love to see them like this.

I went to Vancouver for university. Spencer chose to wait a year. I figured he'd get up to something that would make further schooling redundant. In fact, it was a minor source of shame that I'd trace a more conventional path, majoring in some vague humanity and wandering into the job market. I read about the office spaces of developers in California, where you lounged poolside beneath the fronds. That's where I envisioned Spencer, with an XL black T-shirt and knock-off Oakleys, drinking from a coconut.

The Americans invaded Iraq in my first year. Over MSN, Spencer and I pored over the details. He took a zoomed-out view of it. In quasi-biblical tones, he spoke of civilizations clashing, historical cycles churning, epochs disintegrating. I didn't know where he was absorbing this rhetoric. For me, it was a lot simpler: war was expensive; it had to have a point.

Spencer blamed the balmy West Coast atmosphere for softening my brain.

I wrote, *Isn't it obvious that Rumsfeld is lying?*

And Spencer answered, *Yeah of course.*

For most of my peers, Iraq was the refining flame, solidifying positions on the left or right. Somehow, it worked differently on me. I remember the February 15 protest. I got stuck in a crowd of hippies re-enacting memories of Vietnam marches—walking on stilts, sparking cannons of weed, dressed up like Uncle Sam. The march seemed fun for them, light and playful and nostalgic. Someone on a megaphone read out numbers from protests all around the world: Berlin, 300,000. Barcelona, a million. Rome, another million. There in Vancouver, an estimated 25,000. Everyone cheered; a global passion flowed together. Yet, with startling clarity, I thought we were in error. We were inhabiting a reference, a received idea of dissent.

The protest briefly splintered while a faction, clad in black with red balaclavas, smashed in the windows of a Starbucks. This, too, gestured toward a precursor—I pictured them laughing behind their masks—but I fixed on the desire for violence. The desire was real. That was the spirit, finding its occasion. As the march surged on, I hung around. Broken glass crunched beneath my feet.

After the invasion, I watched Iraqis overrun the statue of Saddam. The media said Americans staged the event, but the violence was ecstatic. The crowds were laughing. No one cared who was behind it or what came next.

—

Not long before I finished my poli sci degree, I got an email from someone named Kim. I had to stare at the name awhile before I realized the message was from Spencer's sister, Kimberley.

She asked if I was coming home for the summer. She said she didn't know how aware I was of the situation. Spencer had been laid off by Bell; he wasn't leaving the basement; she thought he had a problem with his lungs—what their mom once had. He was tired all the time and his legs looked swollen.

I felt embarrassed by her familiar tone, as if, in her mind, I'd only been away a week or two, whereas my entire adult life had unfolded out west. Not that I was avoiding Spencer, but I didn't have time to chat anymore. When I thought about him, that ancient picture in a Palo Alto pool was still parked in my mind, and it came as a shock to realize I might be doing the more remarkable thing with my life.

By then, I was organizing municipal campaigns and advising several provincials. Because of my strident views on foreign intervention, I was generally received as coming from the left, but our campaigns merged affiliations in unclassifiable ways. Push against the edges of the political spectrum, I discovered, and they reach a vanishing point. We never won anything, but we claimed victory whenever another candidate had to answer a question raised by our campaign. Invade the prevailing discourse, we reasoned, and before long, everyone would be living in our world.

But this wasn't a campaign year—I didn't have a candidate—and, in fact, I was planning to go back east that summer. Kim invited me to the house, which their mom had left to them. We had coffee in the living room. I'd never sat there before, always just breezing through on my way to the basement. Every few minutes, I heard Spencer's coughing. Kim said she didn't know what to do anymore; she had to get out of the house, get on with her life. She asked about Vancouver, then seemed to lose focus as I described it.

In a few minutes, I went downstairs. Spencer had the lights off, the room dimly blue from two computer screens. He greeted me as if it hadn't been four years, which made me feel loved. I sat on the edge of the bed. On one screen, he had some chat open; Russian MMA streamed on the other, two women in a bloody knot. He offered me a beer from a mini fridge and coughed.

I asked after his health, and he said, "Black lung."

"Seriously?"

He laughed.

I said that if he was sick, he should've told me sooner.

"Animals hide weakness," Spencer said. "Come on, sit here. I've been wanting to show you something."

One woman drove her knee into the other's spine, but Spencer pointed to the second screen. It was a simple interface, white text clipping down a black box. I recognized certain proper names interspersed with the usual *fap* and *fag*. They were talking politics.

We watched. We laughed together. Sometimes, his laughter ended in coughs. He kept a blanket over his legs.

"We start things here," he said. "Out west, did you ever hear about that third-line goon we got into the All-Star Game?"

My eyes were trained on the text, as if discerning starlight.

"How many of you are there?"

And my best friend said, "More all the time."

The following year, when the Russians beat us in the World Championships, a retired hockey coach named Dom Crossman would make headlines by suggesting that Canada's national vigour was diluted. He singled out certain players; he cited ancient Roman history. Reporters had trouble suppressing smiles. When the *Toronto Star* ran an editorial against him, he said there should be a referendum to decide if the writer should keep her job. Within minutes, the paper's site had crashed.

New faces appear in the green room. Before the convention, they spoke of our campaign as an act of vandalism. Now the president of the party pops an oversized bottle of Veuve Clicquot and toasts Dom Crossman, our nominee.

Even in victory, Wei never stops working. She monitors how many flutes Dom's finished. I bask in the news online, where there's a clearer sense of velocity, even destiny. By contrast, the faces in the green room are as worried as they are celebratory. I only worry they won't go far enough, that this marks the moment Dom becomes one of them. All of a sudden, we've gained a lot of old weight.

"Always on the phone," says the president, who clinks my flute. "Tell me—what are people saying?"

"They're laughing."

"Laughing." She searches my eyes. "I can't tell if you're serious. It's not a pleasant feeling."

I'm about to say, "I had a friend like that," but I keep it to myself.

"Don't sweat it, chief."

The president empties her champagne and looks across the room at Dom. The candidate's face has reddened. Wei hovers at his elbow.

"I've been doing this a long, long time," says the president. "Let me enlighten you. Crossman isn't really one of us. In a federal campaign, people will see that. Be serious for a second—you know he can't win."

I can't hold it any longer. Spencer is here; he's bursting out of us. I break into a smile, and the president reflects it, and now the room fills with laughter.

SARAH CHRISTINA BROWN

LAND OF LIVING SKIES

They were in the papers, on the radio. These girls who, red-faced, with a hardness in their throats, talked about their encounters. Sometimes there were older women too, recounting the sightings they'd once had, but these women were easier to write off because time could cloud their judgment. It was happening everywhere on the continent—in Canada, in California, on tundras, on islands.

People would talk about it on the subway, on the streets. "Did you hear about the latest?" they'd whisper, shifting. I tried not to pay too much attention, but then things began happening in Saskatchewan—the place with a snatched name, the Cree syllables for swift-flowing river whittled down. Radio announcers described the crop circles that had appeared in the yellow fields of durum wheat.

Soon girls were calling in reports on a global scale. Aliens were appearing in their rooms, were leaving wet trails of slime on their skirts. The stories kept coming. It was a new psychological phenomenon, a new hysteria on the horizon.

—

I was far away from the prairie by then. I had moved to the big city and I was working in broadcast television as a news anchor. Men liked to tell me I looked classy, even when I was mouthing their cocks. My big-city men would compare me to actresses from Hollywood's golden era and I got the sense that this was a high compliment. Those women never saw aliens, or if they did they kept it to themselves.

My boss, Dennis, was a buoyant man who subsisted on take-out sandwiches and visions of grandeur for the channel. He had hired me because I was well-spoken, "with good angles," he'd said. I didn't question him on it because truthfully I wasn't quite qualified for the job. But I'd learned quickly enough. Camera left, camera right, cold copy. I was doing fine until he asked me to cover the story. Another crop circle had appeared. There was a cutting edge, an edge to be cut, and we could be close to it.

"Didn't you grow up there?" he asked me.

"Yes," I said, "but to tell you the truth, I barely remember anything at all."

It was a lie, but really, I tried not to think about it too often. I knew it couldn't be much different than anywhere else, but everything was flat there, so it was harder to hide things. Even the sun had nowhere to go, so it spilled down every night like hot lava, like something Martian. And people like to talk in small towns. I'd worked as a waitress at this diner that served all-night milkshakes. Seventy-two flavours and all of them tasted like soap. We were half-sleeping on our midnight-to-morning shift, the air thick with deep-fryer grease, when

Beth, folding her arms across her apron, whispered to me. "My boyfriend," she said, "my boyfriend, he turned into one right in front of me." She'd seen his eyes recede into hollows, his mouth into a hole. "Annie," she said, "in my bed."

We were silent. She bit her lip. Her boyfriend's family owned the province's biggest potash mine, and a lot of people loved him, and they would not like it if she called him an alien. Even the idea, as a joke, would be obscene.

"Should I tell someone?" Her eyes were red, although all of our eyes were red on the night shift. We got so tired. "They'll think I'm crazy."

"I don't know," I said, and although I felt badly about it, I shifted back on my stool. "I mean, are you sure? Was it dark? Maybe you, I mean, could it have been part of a dream?"

Historically, the world had not been good to those who had reported encounters. There was a time when people who saw aliens would be taken away in straitjackets and never seen again. Nowadays society was more liberal, with free speech built into the status quo, but the memories still lingered.

"I mean, I thought I was sure. But maybe. The dark. God, I don't know."

A drunk man came through the front door and demanded a chocolate-cherry marshmallow. The conversation was over. I never brought it up again, and as far as I know, she never told anyone else about what happened.

At work, in what felt like punishment for my passing on the alien story, Dennis assigned me the general-interest segment. It was the last time slot of the hour, and I was meant to interview successful people about their jobs. The majority of these successful people were men. I held microphones out for them. Before the interviews I read dozens of encyclopedic entries on stocks and bonds, science, sports. I had to be very careful about what I said because the slightest slip would mean I wasn't as smart as them. "How do you feel, Robert," I asked a real estate agent in a crisp suit. "How do you feel about interest rates increasing by two point five per cent?"

The nights before I went on television, I slept with my hair in foam rollers that had once belonged to my grandmother. I put a layer of oil on my face and said a little prayer that I would never look old. The woman at the makeup counter had recommended I do this. "Like you're playing Bloody Mary," she'd said, "but, you know, reversed." I said the prayer to my reflection. With my paycheques I had also bought white blouses, black pencil skirts, silk stockings, high heels. I was really a woman. I was a woman living in the big city with a wardrobe and high heels and I was one hundred per cent all right. I was absolved. "I don't live there anymore," I told Dennis when he asked me again about the story. "Please don't ask me again."

Yet the channel was doing okay, despite our mediocre coverage of the alien story. I interviewed a security guard who sent a Slinky down the Eaton's escalator, where it slunk and slunk eternally. "It just keeps going," he said. Crowds formed inside the store for days. So, later that week, I asked if I might take the afternoon off from filming for a doctor's appointment. Dennis was pissed but allowed me to go upon my mention of "women's problems." When I said that, he shut his eyes as though I was about to physically harm him and hissed, "All right!"

I needed a new prescription for my birth control pills, so I put on the paper gown and waited. My new doctor was nice.

Too nice. I made the required complaints about my menstrual cycle to access the prescription, but she waved her hand in pardon and said women were destined for a life of sexual liberation. Like she'd just been thumbing through *Cosmopolitan*. Then she laughed, but her laugh sounded like a sitcom track to me. Something obligatory.

"Now, just lie back and relax. This won't take long."

I tried to relax, but I couldn't. Every time I was in one of these offices, with their sterile smell and blank walls, my body would tense up.

"Does this make you nervous? Maybe pretend it's one of your boyfriends, hah-hah."

I flinched when the thing touched my thigh. It was nothing like a penis, which I generally liked in the right circumstance. It was cold and metallic, like a probe. I immediately wished I could take the thought back. I sat up, almost involuntarily.

The doctor was looking at me curiously.

"Have you ever had contact?"

"What?"

"With extraterrestrial species, I mean."

Was this her idea of bedside manner? "No," I said icily.

"Well, if there's anything you need to discuss . . ."

I shook my head. I laid back down and didn't move one muscle when the cold metal thing went inside me. I wondered if she would add this information to my file, if federal agents would come knocking on my door, if they would pull me into a courtroom and ask me how many times I'd scoured the sky for strange creatures at night. Everything felt like a test. Thank god I had done something with my life; they couldn't suspect me if I had become good at something, I thought. Thank god I'd been on television.

A rival news channel had sent one of their anchors to cover the story. She was also a woman, and somewhere in the prairie outskirts she was interviewing rogue teen girls who wore yellowing flowered fabric over their hair. They were living in a junkyard full of gutted school buses. Fires burned in wheel wells around them, and behind them the land was so open that my breath caught for a second. "Can you tell us what you're wearing?" the anchor asked them.

"These were the bonnets of our great-grandmothers," they said. "They keep the aliens from getting into our heads." The girls sat hand-in-hand in a circle and sang together, pored over familial recipes for flapper pie. "We eat it," they said, "and it takes the aliens out of our bodies. Whatever's left of them in us, it softens." The news was going to have a field day. Already journalists were typing up the headlines. *Live now: flying-saucer-spotting teen freaks!!*

We watched the segment in the back of our newsroom's van. Dennis had brought us all submarine sandwiches and handed them out to us one by one, then switched on the television and said, "Watch." After, he shook his head and sighed. "We're missing out," he said. "We're missing out on quality content. We need to step up our coverage. Big time." It seemed like a speech meant to rouse the whole crew but when he delivered it, he made eye contact only with me.

—

The rival channel may have found the rogue girls, but they still hadn't cracked the crop-circle mystery. "Still haven't!" Dennis would cry every morning, like he was trumpeting a conch shell to unite us. I decided I was really going to throw myself into the general-interest segment. The man I was interviewing that day was a doctor, a dermatologist with his own practice. I did a lot of research about the hidden holes in the sky. Stuff was getting sent up into the atmosphere that did not belong there, and the sun was treacherous in its response. From some latitudes, you could even spot the places where it was beginning to burn through.

"It's hard to spot the warning signs," the doctor said into my microphone. "People can monitor their arms or legs, but what about the parts they can't see?" He told a noble story about cutting a carcinoma from the scalp of a homeless woman, free of charge.

After the interview was finished and the crew had filed out, I noticed the doctor studying my face. He said I had a beauty mark that was worrisome and asked me how much exposure to the elements I'd received. At least he hadn't called it a mole. I told him I'd grown up on a prairie, where sometimes it got so hot the sky opened up and tornadoes came out.

"When was the last time you were fully examined?"

"Oh," I said, "well, never."

"Never?" He was incredulous.

"Well, I don't know, I don't think I'm in danger."

"Please," he said. "These days, everybody is."

The lines on his brow creased. And I thought about how if he didn't do it I'd have to go back to my new doctor, whom I now hated. So I turned my back to him and unbuttoned my blouse.

But what suddenly moved onto me was not at all a human hand but a claw, dripping with slime. I didn't even scream. I just sat there, frozen. And then the doctor was a doctor again, and he was chuckling even, saying *Just part of the checkup* or something like that. From down the hall there was the sound of the cameraman coming back toward the studio. I quickly did up my buttons.

What the hell were you thinking, I later said to myself, taking your blouse off like that? And then—but he was a doctor, and his job, and the sun. And I had seen it, I had felt it, I had felt a claw. Or had I? No, of course I had, but how could it have been that? A *claw*? I felt sick all afternoon. Dennis seemed to sense something was wrong, but to his credit, he didn't press me. He gave me a can of beer on our break, which was a big deal for him. "Now back to work," he said after I swallowed it.

On the plane, the man beside me was reading a newspaper. A crop circle, curved and puckered with the intricacies of an internal organ, was printed on the front page. I was tired yet couldn't sleep. Every time I came close to drifting off I'd look at the man's eye, the half that I could see behind the newspaper. Did it pulsate? No, of course it didn't, but would it soon? Then I'd say to myself, You are insane.

It was as though there was something unearthly inside me now, glowing and insistent, encouraging me to revisit the claw's image. I didn't want to do that, yet I'd thought about it that morning in the shower, when the soap I used felt too much like slime. And I'd thought about it while I said, "Okay, I'll go" to Dennis. He'd nearly choked on his tongue in his haste to purchase the ticket.

As I was trying to sleep, I overheard the stewardess talking to her coworker about their uniforms. "Cold wash and a steam," she said, "and don't forget, on Mondays they like to do girdle checks." I wondered what it was like flying in the sky all the time, so close to whatever else lived in it. Later, seeing I was awake, she came to refill my coffee. "Just us ladies tonight, aren't we?" she asked, gesturing around. I was the only woman in the seats. Most of the other passengers were sleeping peacefully.

The crew drove the rented van toward the place that I'd known before, although I did not know if I'd remember how to get there. But it came back to me quite easily. Two lefts beyond the burnt-down barn. When we stood in the middle of the flattened field, it felt like all the air had been sucked down.

Our plan, which was not much, was to sit there and wait for whoever was making the crop circles to show themselves. Other channels had tried this before, but Dennis was banking on my familiarity with the place, as though my connection to the prairie would compel the aliens to show themselves. "Give the viewers the inside scoop," he instructed. "Tell them what it's like to stand there. Pretend you're interviewing yourself." Now that I was here, I could see for myself how fully ridiculous our plan was.

Yet as the crew unwound cables to set up the camera, my eye caught something on the periphery of the circle. Where the wheat grew tall again, I could suddenly make out the outline of a girl, pressing a stalk down with her toe.

"Look, over there," I said to the cameraman. He looked, squinting.

"I don't see anything," he said. Now there was nothing there. I realized I had seized his arm, and I let go abruptly.

"I'm sorry," I said. "I'm tired."

He shrugged.

We waited. I needed to think of an informative hook to start off my broadcast, so I contemplated the nature of the crop circle. Why were their signs coded in this indecipherable language, like they enjoyed making a mystery out of it? It would be so much less complicated if an alien would show up and claim responsibility for the circle, rather than making the rest of us scramble around, feet in the dirt, figuring it out. Maybe, if we stood out here long enough, one would come. I crossed my fingers. I did not want to lose my job.

Another hour went by. The crew was getting bored and hungry and, with apologetic looks, they asked me if they could go find some food. "Fine. Go get a milkshake from that diner we passed," I told them. "It'll wash your mouth out."

"Radio us if something happens," the cameraman yelled from the van as they drove away.

I stood in the middle of the circle. I'd brought the encyclopedia, even though the crew had teased me about it. Now I turned the page to circle (*crop*). The encyclopedia cautioned the reader against believing aliens had made the circles. More likely, it said, they were made by humans, for attention-seeking, or to give significance to a particular place.

Dennis radioed me from our hotel. I was almost glad to hear his voice. "You're doing it, kid," he said. "Groundbreaking stuff."

I said, "Yeah, yeah," and hung up.

The sun was sinking down. Soon it would touch the circle's edge, and perhaps what I thought I'd seen would appear again. The girl. That was impossible, unless it wasn't. Who knew which girls were here now or what they did.

Of course, as girls, we played that game here. Hide-and-seek. We'd hide from one another in the wheat, hands over our mouths to mask our breath while another girl pushed through with arms outstretched, calling our names. I always hated being the seeker. I'd open my eyes and see nothing but soft amber, so many stalks. The smell became nauseating in its sweetness. I'd walk forward and find only more of it, rustling. But then it would come—the sight of a hand or flash of hair, just enough to spot within the thick, fringed field. I'd find them. Or they'd burst out themselves, flattening the stalks with the force of their reveal, and there would be screams, a chorus of them.

I can't remember the age we stopped playing. We got better at hiding, so it no longer felt like a game.

The camera sat there staring at me. I knew I was supposed to talk about the circle, but I didn't know how. What could I say? For a time, my knowledge of aliens had come through our rabbit-eared TV. Those ones were cartoonish and green, clownish with antennae. They dragged their captives into huge ships. They said things like *Take me to your leader!* and salivated.

What I'd learned was different. Strangeness could be there one minute, gone the next. Shapes shifted, faces changed. I had no names for all these things, so I took my good-angled face and angled it away from them.

Now, facing the camera, I thought about how the word was designed to make people turn away from it. Alien. It tinged everything with suspicion. Every time I said it, it felt terrible in my mouth. There were no aliens appearing before me, no girl; the only thing I could see was the sky. This whole time I'd been living under the same one, but I'd convinced myself it looked different if I moved around. Dennis would not be happy to learn this, but I now understood it didn't. It was all the same thing no matter where you stood, and it was big enough that you couldn't ever really see it fully.

BEN LADOUCEUR

A BOY OF GOOD BREEDING

Hank draws a line down Jerry's body, bottom lip to penis tip. The line is made of slobber, drawn with his tongue, and almost straight, detouring only for the scar on Jerry's lower stomach. Hank always goes out of his way to touch the scar, to communicate that everything of Jerry's belongs in his, Hank's, mouth, even the parts that speak of damage.

There is no music playing in the room, but an assonance rings in both of their ears, serving to remind them that they were just at a nightclub, where the music was very loud, because conversation was not the idea in that place. The idea was dancing, and being seen, and being considered beautiful. This deafness is a sensation Hank is accustomed to. Jerry is not accustomed to it, for he normally stays home while Hank goes out and does the things he finds fun.

Jerry should have stayed home this evening. He could have opted out like he always does, half-heartedly citing a sore throat, or maybe an unmissable hockey game. That wouldn't be plausible, since the playoffs just wrapped up, but Hank doesn't know these things. "What's Edmonton's team called?" Jerry had once asked flirtatiously, about a year ago, back when the differences between them were still fascinating instead of unnerving, explored instead of unaddressed.

"Whale sharks," Hank had answered. Then they'd both laughed.

But tonight, Jerry came out to the club, thinking, vaguely, that it would be his last chance to do so, before leaving.

Leaving what? The apartment, Hank, the city? Again, the thought was vague.

Hank always calls Jerry's hometown *the sticks*, as though he grew up in a hut made of sticks, and dragged a long stick against stick-fences every morning on his way to a school made of sticks, wherein he ate sticks for lunch, earthy with dirt and sticky with sap. When they'd first met, the word *faggot* was still in Jerry's vocabulary. He'd used it to describe people who littered and hockey players who missed easy goals. Hank would always remind him that a faggot was a bundle of sticks. To this, Jerry would reply, "Sticks and stones will break my bones," as a weird little nothing joke, behind which lay a private truth. Jerry was under the impression, at that time, that words could never hurt him.

They'd met in a room in which Jerry had not been certain if he was allowed to swear. There had been a bookshelf erupting with overflow, a fancy green lamp, a giant desk between the two men, and a silence like that of a library. Hank's chair was tufted and leather; Jerry's was plastic, uncomfortable, and meant for impermanent people. He was there for help with an essay. It was still the beginning of the school year.

"I picked English as a major because I liked it in high school," he said to Hank, who would be his tutor for the next twenty minutes. "But it's so much work. So many ways to fuck it up. Sorry. Screw it up."

"You can swear here," said Hank, with a lilt in his voice. "This is a place where you can swear, Mr. . . ." Then Hank read Jerry's name from the university database, his whole name—*Jeremiah Voth*. But Jerry told Hank to call him Jerry, as he tells everyone to do.

Months later, Hank would ask if he could call Jerry *Jeremiah* after all, for he found the name mellifluous, like a silky ribbon pulled out of the mouth, between the front teeth. Jerry was okay with this, although he suspected it was a sort of fetishizing of his Mennonite childhood, full of wooden toys and institutional racism and joyrides with thirteen-year-olds at the wheel, and girls you closed your eyes to kiss. It was interesting if you weren't there. It was interesting to Hank, and still is.

After their tutoring appointment that day, they'd encountered each other again at the Starbucks nearby. Following Hank's instruction, Jerry was reading the novel about which he had to write an essay within the next forty-eight hours. He had gone through two coffees and was only on page twenty-five. He had never read this much literature in one day.

The café was crowded, so Hank asked if he could share his table. That was when Jerry realized he recognized Hank's face from posters around campus. In them, Hank was shirtless and in the arms of another man, who had long blond hair. Both men wore lipstick in the photos. There was text across their arms and chests, information about some event, and a title near their heads. Now, working on his third coffee, Jerry said this title out loud, to the man he had seen shirtless everywhere.

"Animal Uproar," he said and smirked.

"Oh, yes. That's me. A little embarrassing. But that's what I do. Not for money. I tutor for money. But acting is what I do."

Now Hank saw how little of the book Jerry had gotten through.

"Look," he said, "I felt weird about giving you this advice in the office, but I'll say it now—just read the beginning and the end. The rest you can get away with skipping. Read the first twenty pages, then the last twenty. You don't have time to finish the book. The gist will do."

There were months of togetherness between that night and this one. But those are in the middle, and Jerry skips it. If he reflects, he reflects on the beginning that took place so long ago, and the end that is taking place currently. An unread novel, a trail of slobber. *The rest you can get away with skipping.*

Jerry failing the essay about the book. Failing more essays. *Skip it.* Losing his room in residence, and not even noticing, having moved his guitar and clothes and laptop charger into Hank's apartment. *Skip it.* Hank in a pair of his, Jerry's, briefs, shimmying in his sleep like a dog that is dreaming of running. Hank in bright clothing, on his way somewhere. Hank getting up at night to write something down. Hank in the dark. Hank in his moods. Move along. Nothing to see here. *Skip.* Jerry drinking at bars alone, to watch the games. Coming home to find Hank plastered too. Smoking less but not quitting. Realizing he'd been in Toronto for six months and was yet to make any friends, aside from this dog-man sleeping beside him. Telling Hank about his upbringing, his mother, his near-death from colitis, the months he'd spent bedridden in buttfuck nowhere; Hank always listening carefully.

Using Hank's pepper spray, thinking it was breath spray. It tasted nothing like pepper.

Why did Hank have that in his satchel? Jerry asked with his eyes, his voice being out of commission.

"Because maybe the world will see me and hate me," said Hank as he brought water to Jerry, who was crumpled against the toilet, spitting peppery vomit or vomiting peppery spit. It was difficult to say. "And maybe," Hank continued, "it will be late at night when that happens. And there will be more of them than of me. That's life."

Not Jerry's life. But he chose to say nothing here. Everything was difficult to say. Physically and mentally. *You can get away with skipping this.* Jerry skips it, and now he is getting away.

Tonight, Hank is drawing a line down Jerry's body, thin and invisible. The skin underneath the line is colder than the skin to either side of it. It is nice that the two of them can fuck like teenagers, can find each other's bodies, their lengths, their hairs, their heats, so neat. For Jerry, this must be the effect of a teenagehood spent in the arms of females, toward whom he'd felt a strange, unwelcome, ignored emotion that he was later able to identify as indifference. Hank, on the other hand, has had male bodies near, against, all over his own, many times before. Nonetheless, something about their sex is wild to Hank too. Hank's eagerness, as such, must originate from elsewhere. Not Jerry's maleness. There is some other component found new and exciting by Hank.

Jerry believes he has finally learned from where.

For months, Hank has been working on a new play, called *A Boy of Good Breeding*. He wrote it himself, and his friend Odie is the director. Until recently, all that Jerry knew about it was that, for every show, a basket of apples had to be purchased. Hank described the script as boring. "But the story chugs along and really, it's all about the space, the movement, the humans. You have to just *see* it," Hank said.

The *you* here was not Jerry, but people in general. Jerry did not attend Hank's plays. Hank, he has since learned, depended on this.

Why did he never attend them? Because of the one time he did go, and they both learned that it was not a good idea. This is from the middle of their story; Jerry recollects it now, but quickly.

That play, the one that Jerry attended, was called *Deepest Darkest*. On the walk home, they'd both smoked. Hank had wanted to know, what did Jerry think?

He was sure it was good, but to be honest, to him, it was just a bit weird.

Well, Jerry had missed some things then. Did he not pick up on the subtext? Hank would be happy to explain it a little. "Remember the housewife my character kept visiting? We weren't just friends. I was having an affair with her."

"Oh, I see," said Jerry. "It's just that I thought your character was gay."

The conversation stopped. Apparently, Hank had not intended for his character to be gay, but could not help that voice, that *way* of his. Jerry had just spoken to the invisible border surrounding Hank, on the other side of which stood heroes, husbands, heartthrobs—meaty roles in real productions. On the other side of which stood also an easier life, one that merited less pepper spray.

Jerry was embarrassed to have said something so hurtful, but within that embarrassment was genuine surprise. Hank really couldn't turn it off. Go figure. More words would come from Hank that night, angry and shaky, but not for hours. Instead of words, their mouths for the moment formed smoke.

Two plays followed during which Jerry stayed at home. But after the first performance of *A Boy of Good Breeding*, Hank had asked Jerry how he pronounced *stoma*. This had piqued Jerry's interest, so he attended the show, earlier this evening, without telling Hank that he would.

Jerry had previously wondered how Hank ever managed to fund his productions. Now he understood that there was very little money involved. There were no real costumes, and the cast was small. Each actor played more than one character, except for one, whose hair was blond like Jerry's, whose limbs were long like Jerry's, whose character's name was a lot like Jerry's. Obediah.

Obediah was a dolt, and his life among the Mennonites was idyllic. Much more idyllic than the real thing had been for Jerry, when he was actually living it rather than watching a poor simulacrum unfold on a stage. In the first scene, Obediah's mother smashed apples with her fists upon learning that he'd decided to leave for the city. Yes, that had happened in Jerry's real life, but she hadn't been such a gorilla about it. Her wrinkles, too, were heavier-set, not mere mascara scratched across the face of a crotchety ingenue.

In the next scene, Obediah rolled his shirt up, showing the scar on his stomach from the stoma. He pontificated on trauma—the venom in his system, the night he'd almost died, how torturous it was to have a faulty body there is no escape from, to wake up and find that your colostomy bag has ripped and filled the bed with your own shit.

When had Jerry told Hank that story? He would not have done so easily. Hank, with his soft voice and well-timed coos of encouragement, had drawn so many stories out of Jerry. Now those words were here, on stage—but multiplied by ten. His life was only suffering, sticks and stones, in the eyes of the author.

After curtains, he brought Hank the flowers he had purchased beforehand.

"Oh. Jeremiah. You saw it."

"Yes."

"What did you think?"

"A little familiar."

"Yes, I suppose," replied Hank. *Everything of you belongs to me* was the sentence that could have followed. The *you* here not denoting people in general, but Jerry in particular.

Following the production, Hank was off to the Village with some of the cast, and that was when Jerry decided to go along.

Most of Hank's pals were strangers to him, so quickly did the people in Hank's social circle seem to arrive and depart. Tonight, they were, for the most part, chilly but aloof. They liked Jerry when they learned he was a smoker; conversations on the heated patio were boozy and buoyant and manageable. But back at the bar, they started helping themselves to the cigarettes he kept in his backpack, and they did not invite him to come outside with them.

He drank while Hank danced, though he spent more time watching the Obediah actor, who moved to the music as though it were an extension of himself. Jerry approached him from the bar, leaving his chaser behind, and grabbed Obediah as though he was his. He kept hold of him, closing in, pressing back against chest, mouth against neck. He wanted the air between them gone. He wanted them as one.

Obediah pried himself away. Jerry fought deeper through the crowd and found Hank's mouth, over which he put his own. Then he said, "We're going home," and here they are now, home safe and sound and undressed, post-coital, pre-cleanup, four arms and four legs in a mess of a braid.

Here's what will happen tomorrow. To get rid of their hangovers, they will walk to St. Lawrence Market, as they often do if it isn't raining. It being a Saturday, there will be trinkets for sale instead of perishable goods, which are there on Sundays. So, rather than buying muffins and cups of four-dollar coffee, they will meander through the aisles of paperbacks, antiques, doilies in plastic sheets, and ceramic mugs with charming imperfections and asymmetries. Hank will keep his sunglasses on, even in the market hall, in order to give the impression of suffering, of dehydration, of a Friday night spent with the cool kids.

They will come upon a typewriter. Hank will show an interest, and type a few keys on the page that has been placed there. Among the curse words and the rows of same letters over and over—*aaaaaaa, zzzzzzz*—Hank will type promotional information about his play, which runs for another two weeks. He will type the time, the place, the price. He will long for a typewriter like this, all loud and clunky. He will express interest in becoming a typewriter person, keeping the neighbours awake all night by making art. But he will not buy the typewriter.

Jerry will go to the bathroom to defecate, as he does every hour or so after a night of drinking. He will return to the typewriter, and see that Hank is now farther down the aisle, poking through books. Jerry will purchase the typewriter and bring it to Hank as a gift. Hank will do a double take.

"Where will we keep it?" Hank will ask, for the bachelor apartment they share is tiny.

"Don't sweat it," Jerry will reply, a thing he never says without meaning it.

Hank will then kiss him on the side of the lip, even though public displays of affection make Hank's palms sweaty for a reason he has never disclosed to Jerry.

As they walk out of the market, Hank will deduce the reason Jerry told him not to worry about space. The reason is that there will soon be plenty of space in the apartment, for Jerry is not long for this apartment, this city, this life. Jerry will have brought Hank to such an understanding without having to find the words. The words were elusive, they weren't words yet, and they never would be, they were phonemes, methane, theories. Words are not Jerry's thing. It always takes too much out of him, forming them.

The conversation will be unexpectedly quiet. Hank will cry behind his sunglasses and maintain his composure. He will not plead or scream, but, feeling newly free of the emotional obligations of a lover, he will tell Jerry many, many hurtful things. He will, in his anger, reach for all the most devastating criticisms of Jerry's life and personality, uttering carnages that Jerry will remember verbatim for decades. As he does this, he will demand cigarette after cigarette from Jerry, lighting each with the tip of the last.

With the typewriter, he will write another play about Jerry, who will not attend the production. Jerry will be living and working in Fort McMurray by the time it is staged. He will come upon a trailer for the play while browsing Hank's Facebook page, a habit of his, Fort Mac being a lonely and heterosexual space. He won't be out of the closet there; nobody will suspect it, and it'll never come up.

He'll watch that trailer many times, on many nights. It will be, at once, sad and pleasant, moving through those months again, but this time from a distance, as part of the audience.

ANGÉLIQUE LALONDE

POOKA

Pooka lived in a room with carpets of all shapes and sizes woven from different cloths. Pooka picked up carpets wherever he went. Most of the time unwanted carpets were dirty or cut up or had cigarette burns in them or smelled like cat piss, so Pooka had a lot of cruddy carpets alongside the nice carpets he was gifted or able to buy during blowout sales at home furnishing stores, end-of-the-roll off-sales, and Oriental outlets. He mixed them together because Pooka was like that, all mixed up himself. Off-white blend of kinfolk peppered down the line. Indian nearly fractioned out, they told him, because Grand-maman Therése, already a half-breed, married Renaud Fortier, a Frenchman from the logging camp upriver. Then Mama took up with Gunther Poundsly, Pooka's no-good pa who gave only bruises, crooked teeth, a penchant for sauerkraut, and armfuls of meanness until he left them to go back to the Sault.

Mama said, "getting lighter with each successive generation of mixing"; said, "despite blending in, the ghosts of the ancestors are all frayed up inside, calling to our spirits with directions we don't know how to follow, so we get lost along the way."

Frayed up from not knowing how to live between worlds, Pooka knew—from the structural forgettings legislated on Mama and Grand-maman's lives, and the oceans between here and the places in the world his other people came from. Mama did some big forgetting, she said, when she was twelve years old and the government came to take her out of the bush, place her in a good white home where there wasn't no more booze, just a whole lot of work, a brother who liked to touch her up, and godliness she shed as soon as she skipped out at sixteen. Didn't see Grand-maman again until Gunther left and the city streets spat her out, back to the village with her little boy. Not-quite-white Pooka, picked on at powwow for his white-boy face, ticking the Métis box on the Census 'cause that was the closest fit. Nevermind that saying it out loud made him feel like a sham, bringing up everything he didn't know about who he was supposed to be.

Pooka felt there was no real demarcation between things. He learned from his school books that life was a mash-up of history told like a storybook of happy endings if you were on the right side and unfortunate circumstances that couldn't be reversed now if you weren't. He knew that the sullied carpets he collected had been woven from pristine cloth, that given time and human use the new carpets would become sullied. For Pooka, the mixed-up rugs felt something like a homeland. A place to collapse time and storylines, create a sanctified present from a mucked-up past.

The rugs were Pooka's only furnishings. Layered and layered on each other to make a bed or a rise on which to set a coffee mug. Sometimes Pooka got creative and sculpted them into intricate replicas of couches he sat on at other people's houses.

Once, during a particularly bleak winter, he sculpted an entire IKEA bedroom suite. The lampshade was a bit tricky, and although he was usually loath to do so, for this particular project he got hold of a pair of scissors. He cut up one of the already-torn carpets so that the lampshade would fit right and not light on fire from pieces of fabric touching the bulb. He looked up videos of how to wire a lamp on YouTube and scavenged wiring from a lamp of Cousin Vicky's. It made Pooka feel modern to have a lamp in his home, to live in an IKEA bedroom suite like all the women he met who worked at smart retail stores, the only ones other than Cousin Vicky who would talk to him.

Pooka spent a lot of time in smart retail stores pretending to shop for things. Mostly he was getting ideas for how to sculpt his carpets, or noticing display carpets showing wear that might come on sale sometime soon because no one would want to pay full price for them. Pooka knew how to talk carpet; he could always haggle the saleswomen down. With sales-men he didn't even bother, feeling most of the time like they weren't worth the trouble of talking rug with. They wanted to seal the deal, not send the carpet to a good home. Or so Pooka thought.

Pooka was thrilled when his room of sculpted carpets was featured on a website. One of those sites where people who spend a lot of time on computers go to compare their own lives to those of other people they have never met who live in places like New York or San Francisco. Meaningful places with panache that people might imagine themselves in. Online mock-ups for how to navigate the world of things and properly curate a life. His "eclectic suite," however, was quickly taken down because of the spiteful putdowns posted by viewers who were used to staged, minimalistic homes. Homes that displayed their inhabitants' sophistication, cookie-cutter individuality, and eye for tasteful decor. Homes that had class.

"This place looks like a thrift store stocked by a blind four-year-old," wrote Micah4u. "Is this a joke?" posted dEsignBaby. "This is the most tasteless jumble of trash I've ever seen in my life," was Grendel Piker's response.

Pooka was crushed. This was during his 1960s *Star Trek* phase, when he'd actually gone so far as to spray-paint some of his carpets silver and black to look like Captain Kirk's chair. His photographer friend Peanut, who had taken the artful photos of Pooka's rug replica of the bridge of the USS *Enterprise* (NCC-1701), felt awful about the ordeal.

Pooka pretended not to care about what online design critics thought of the place he called home. He reckoned they couldn't see beyond the obvious, viewing things only in terms of outlines and not in terms of spirit. He saw that theirs was a gated community of taste, that they used aesthetic condemnation to keep the riff-raff out. Nonetheless, Pooka dismantled the carpet rendition of Captain Kirk's bridge.

Until then Pooka's fanciful successes in carpet sculpture had helped to keep his mind off Mama's latest disappearance, let him keep pretending she was just drifting, that like every other time she had drifted before, she would find her way home. But time stretched on and Mama did not resurface. With nothing to distract him, Pooka's heart broke. Pooka knew this time that Mama was lost, the way Tante Bernadette was lost, and Tina from high school, and Liz from the village upriver. No follow-up down at the station, no mention on the evening news or photos along the roadside. One more woman washed out of a world scripted to efface her, not even a ripple in the surface of the fabricated story in which all people belong.

Pooka's online ridicule was one more disappointment in a life he could only see through his sorrows. Alone on the outskirts of his humanity, not belonging became too much for Pooka. He ceased pretending to be Mr. Spock, wearing pointy ears and trying all sorts of foreign foods he found around town to test the Vulcan's taste buds. He couldn't remember what Grand-maman had said about always being at home among his ancestors because he could not speak their tongues and had no sense of the inspirited landscapes they'd inhabited. He could not hear them because they were far gone to him, people in history books wearing clothing crafted from animal skins, weaving baskets and boxes from plants. Pioneers with fringe jackets and musket rifles, bottom-of-the-barrel Englishmen sailing in the bowels of dank ships, German peasants tilling up whatever land they could find, uprooting hundred-year-old trees with bare hands.

Pooka's sneakers were made in China by labourers he'd never know, his skin clothed in factory cotton travelled all around the globe, though he'd barely been a hundred klicks from the one-room box he called home. Unlike Grand-maman, Pooka couldn't hear the ancestors when he walked through the furniture district downtown built atop the old fish camps.

But sometimes Pooka imagined that the carpets gave voice to them, that the foreign-made rugs hoarded up in showrooms scattered all over the city might be a medium through which the relations could speak. The IKEA suite and bridge of the *Enterprise* were Pooka's attempts at coaxing them out.

After Pooka's online ventures in "carpArtry" were quashed, and with Mama gone for good this time, he became unable to feel at home among his carpets. For five years Pooka kept things flat. He didn't shop around or notice shifting trends in rug manufacturing. He lost track of developments in loom engineering and stopped haggling for deals altogether. Pooka was down-and-out. During these years Pooka worked on and off as a casual labourer for various construction projects. He experimented with crystal meth and got addicted to it, the way people do. He made other meth friends who were down-and-out like him. A lot of scattered spirits stimulated only by the hit, every other aspect of life losing texture, ceasing to impart meaning.

His den became littered with drug paraphernalia, unwashed dishes, and dirty laundry he couldn't bother to clean. Pooka lost sense of himself. He couldn't find space in his heart for the things that had once fed him, even though he finally had a girlfriend who cooked for him: bowls of pasta with sauce from a jar and broken light bulbs of crystal. Poor little messed-up Mel, who went into fits of rage when his attention went elsewhere.

When he wasn't high, and often when he was, Pooka laboured on the infrastructure for modern condos downtown, making sure to always leave jobs before getting to the interiors.

Pooka didn't want anything to do with the insides people would inhabit. He always took special care not to go into the show suites because of the shame they brought up in him about his loss of inspiration. Because they highlighted how clean people would live, people who weren't like him and couldn't understand the depths of his degradation, his loneliness, and all the ways he'd been hard done by in this world. Never-loved-properly Pooka crouching inside the cupboards, Papa smashing pots overhead in the sink muttering about his uselessness.

Things would have gone on like this if it weren't for the special set of circumstances that sheared the fuzz from Pooka's synapses. They would have gone on like this until desperation led to violence, incarceration, bodily breakdown, or just plain giving up. Pooka was often up in the ironworks; it would not have been difficult to fall. Only the thought of his carpets kept him from inching off the edge, the thought of the voices trapped up in them that might be lost forever if he didn't arrange them into perceivable forms. Pooka knew for certain they'd be thrown into a trash bin by his landlord, who would find them filthy, even cringe at the thought of them, when he'd recount the story of having to haul out Pooka's decrepit stacks.

It was a deconstruction project in the warehouse district on the industrial fringes of the city that finally bridged Pooka's mind and heart. A complex of concrete blocks that had been abandoned and boarded up since before Pooka had moved to the city. The faded lettering on the awning illegible in the grimy expanse of a neighbourhood you only went to if you had something specific to get at one of the duct ventilation or fire safety supply stores.

Pooka walked into what was once Desislava's Authentic Eastern Imports gritty and wanting, his heart like the sandpaper tongue of a mother cow licking flies off her just weaned calf across the wire, risking the electric shock just to get some closeness. Frazzled, murky Pooka, just this side of the meth binge that had started as a helluva time but finally broke him and Mel, leaving him friendless on the other side.

Pooka didn't notice what was all around him in the dim light until he felt a full-bodied cushioning rise up through the soles of his steel-toed boots. He started, recognizing the somatic resonance of a nineteenth-century Chiprovtsi kilim. He dropped to his knees to examine the fibres, running his labour-roughened hands along the weft of the red and black threads. Pooka knew this was authentic Bulgarian, could sense in the filaments an outpouring of nationalistic sentiment from just after the Crimean War. He looked up and saw an entire storeroom of rolled and stacked rugs, dotted here and there with statuettes, vases, and urns, coated with rubble from the collapsing roof and dank from water damage at the southeast end. Pooka woke up, snapped into consciousness as if charged by an electric current running through an otherwise inert substance. He returned to his being amid Desislava's abandoned relics, receptors in his brain sensing joy from something other than methamphetamine for the first time in years.

"The whole lot of it's for the dump," said Boss Slims, who'd hired him to do the job.

There on the kilim, Pooka sensed he'd been called upon to salvage what he could of the ruins of Desislava's treasures, precious emblems of foreign cultures cast upon his shores.

He asked Slims if he could take some of the wreckage home instead of tossing it out.

"So long as you ain't turning a profit I don't see no issue with it," said Slims. "I got the call from City Hall to haul it to the trash yard before they tear it down. Don't see as anyone would mind you sifting through, so long as there ain't anything shady you intend to do with it."

He paused and Pooka twitched, both from anxiety—that he might have to resort to criminal pillage to take the kilims home if Slims didn't agree to it—and the neurotoxic effects of meth withdrawal.

"There was some kind of scandal that ended this place up in the courts some while back, so it might be someone's keeping an eye out," Boss Slims recalled.

"It was in the papers but I can't recollect the details, maybe deportation or tax fraud. No one could liquidate 'til they cleared up the ownership. In '97 or '98 we got that real bad winter with the ice storms and frost heaves, come spring there was a crack clear through the back wall. Water's been seeping for years, no one allowed in to do anything about it. All this junk left to rot. Mould and rat shit all over the place. Can't see there's anything worth anything left, but you might find something worth keeping. Must've been a fortune here at some point."

Pooka told Boss Slims it was for an art project. Slims looked at him cockeyed, unsure about the kind of art Pooka'd make out of this mess. He told him to be discreet, not to go showing things off or anything, seeing as someone might recognize the material if they were looking for it. Pooka said he'd be selective, dump most of what was there like he was supposed to, and transform what he took beyond recognition so no one could trace things back.

Pooka lives in a room lined with carpets of all shapes and sizes and colours woven into different forms. Six years Pooka's had with the detritus of Desislava's big dreams. Six years keeping himself clean by tending to the discards of someone else's life and in so doing reimagining his own. Pooka has moved beyond stacking now, daring to dream beyond the confines of an inherited reality. Pooka unravels threads and weaves new images, reinterpreting the past. In the new tapestries, Pooka's mama lives in a nest edged by curlicues and red-leafed maples. She comes and goes as she pleases and no harm can reach her. He weaves her as a hawk, like in the stories she used to tell him. Pooka remembers that Mama loved him once, before a bad life got hold of her spirit, broke her wings, and boxed her into a story she could not live out.

Pooka is joyful for Mama, joyful to tell her story the way she wanted it told. He drapes her on his back and carries her to the shore to watch the waves come in, to be held in by her ancient warmth.

The act of unravelling releases the knots that ruptured the ancestor's storylines, fraying them up so that Pooka could not hear them, could feel only the schism of loss. Pooka's whole being is immersed in the work of untangling, and even though he doesn't always know what the voices of the ancestors are saying as he takes apart and remakes, he hears their joy and is able to feel hope. They come to him as if in dreams, ancestors who feel the wind in their hair, haul fish up from the river, same river out the window, same water that wetted the ancestors' tongues, upon which they travelled. Pooka envisions the wind, allowing it to tickle the water; frissons of blue, green, and white dotted here and there with the bright silver flashes of fish coming home, souls waiting to be reborn. Streaks of grey and brown amid the red and yellow flush of autumn, faces open to the wind as they transition between this life and the next, passing through death along the way.

This form, this life, the structure of reality that smashed him up on the inside, made his mother-folk fade in and out. Made the world a mismatch of other people's stories he could not claim as his own, his father-folk a frenetic aching coursing through his fingers. Pooka sees the holes and loops and presses love into them, easing the passage to rooms where people talk and their voices are the clacking sounds of branches and migratory birds, kinships of forest, field, fowl, fingers tapping out a tune.

Pooka builds bridges between heartbreak and happiness. Bridges to cross over his fear. Safe passage for a cluttered soul hiding out to escape the bang-up job Papa did on his life, the system always pressing in to keep him down. He guts the gutters where he's lived so long among the effluents of a world that doesn't want him. He finds brethren there and gives them new forms. As he re-stories rugs, Pooka becomes a maker of worlds instead of a castoff living within the confines of his shame. Reworking threads reroutes his neural pathways. Bit by bit new patterns emerge, healing wounds rather than wearing them raw over and over and over again.

Pooka gathers plants in city parks, along sidewalks, and in the forest edging the ends of bus lines. He lends colours to bleached-out strands: alder bark and wild carrot root for orange, blackberries for purple, lichens for red and yellow, birch bark for brown. He uproots beets from the community gardens to coax a deep red, fixing the dye with vinegar from packets picked up at A&W. Blacks he gets from walnut hulls, staining his hands at the same time, and greens from nettles and peppermint that he also brews into tea. Plants, creatures, and new geographies of colour teach him to sing the songs of the city as his ancestors learned to sing the songs of the land.

Still, this is not a success story to print in magazines read by all the women who work at smart retail stores. Pooka has not remade his identity and turned his life around to become a better version of himself. He has not stepped out of destitution into a life of blissful hope. Despite his efforts, Pooka's threads sometimes lead to despair. His ancestors' sufferings and cruelties, Mama's missing face smiling at him from tattered photographs, Tante Bernadette, Tina, Papa's big fists, and all the traumas of life are there in the mouldy patches of Desislava's rugs. Are there in the morning when he wakes up and everything he loves has been distorted into ugliness or taken from him, hindering his heart. Pooka is often unable to build the bridges needed to traverse his emptiness. Sometimes the way out is not clear. The old ruts in his mind are mighty worn and he longs for a simple wormhole of dopamine to flood him into peace. Even though time after time these quick clicks to happiness have only led to the same sad place.

Pooka tricks himself into presence by delving into the enlivened materiality of the kilims. String by string he weaves himself into place, his fingers unravelling the fabrics of other official histories. He finds hope there for other ways of telling. He'll tie one knot, make a loop, cut here, and the fray of the thread will suggest another pattern. This is no ideal world, fabric constrained by the genesis of its being and former lives, but what is woven can be teased apart. Pooka tampers and tugs at reality, drawing it by hand, creating new pathways through the made-up world.

SAMANTHA JADE MACPHERSON

THE FISH AND THE DRAGONS

China, at night, on the river. My grandfather was a master fisherman and he did it the old way, with cormorants. Each night, fourteen dark birds perched on the gunwales of his wooden boat, not idle passengers, but crew as well. Often he took me with him. I stood in the bow and held the lantern to illuminate the water. Also to attract the fish. We would glide through gloom, quiet except for the dip of the long bamboo pole Grandfather used to propel us, the ruffle of stiff feathers, the hum of crickets on the far shore. Still except for the movement of the boat, the breeze against Grandfather's loose shirt, stained pants rolled to knee.

Fishing with cormorants took great skill and required the fisherman to trust his birds completely, as Grandfather did. With wrinkled hands he offered pieces of chopped carp, and their beaks snatched at him and asked for more. Even on their perches, wings tucked against sides, they scrutinized my grandfather with bright eyes. The birds looked for food perhaps, or attention, but I watched his slight figure with the fascination of a boy who has not known his father.

He began each night by tying snares around the birds' necks to prevent them from swallowing the catch. To do this, he would hold the bird still and slip a knotted hemp rope around the base of its throat. Not so tight it couldn't fish, but snug enough the catch remained trapped in the cavity below the beak. Thus outfitted, he released his birds to the river. Others chose to attach thin lines to the feet of their birds, but Grandfather's cormorants didn't require a tether. They swam wide circles around our boat and dived without warning. One moment bobbing on the surface and the next fully submerged. When they caught a fish, Grandfather guided them to the boat with his pole and forced the birds to regurgitate their prey by massaging their necks, thumbs pointed upward. He kept the catch, rewarded the birds with a small piece of meat, and sent them out again. We caught many fish this way.

When I was seven, Grandfather showed me how to gut carp. Despite the difficulty of working on an unstable surface, we did it onboard, while fishing. The twelve-foot vessel had wooden slats across the middle to provide structure, but still it wobbled. Flat-bottomed, only the ends of the boat curled away from the water. Not seaworthy, but sufficient for our placid river. Grandfather held the slimy fish in his hand to demonstrate. Its recent death still perfumed the air around us, the scent of fresh fish before any hint of decay could mar it, strangely appealing. The birds continued to circle the boat. Unrelenting in their pursuit, they appeared and disappeared, like visitors in a constant state of flux. I could not keep track of their movements nor discern any semblance of pattern. "Always keep your knife sharp," Grandfather said. "The cuts must be clean." He gutted quickly, without looking, and made only the essential slits. His hands moved with casual confidence and economy developed over years of repetition. Finished, he doused the flayed fish in a bucket to clean the blood. "See," he said. "Easy."

Not easy. The fish nearly slipped from my hands when Grandfather passed it to me. I propped it between my knees. The knife went in smoothly. With blade in fish and wooden grip in hand, I felt like a seven-year-old assassin. Shadowy as a legend, perhaps on a quest from a long-dead emperor. I looked toward Grandfather for approval, but he was intent on his work, pulling a bird back to the boat with his pole. He looked old and crooked, next to that fishing pole. Bent back, white hair, and teeth blackened at the gums. All of him was wrinkled and I wondered, perhaps as you wonder about me now, how long he would last. I pushed the knife too hard. It slid through white carp flesh and into my thumb. The fish fell from my hand. Hot blood dripped on the wooden slats and spattered at my feet.

Grandfather abandoned his bird and grabbed my hand. Squinting, he pulled the cut open and examined it under yellow lamplight. "Suck on it," he said. "It's not bad." In my mouth the metallic tang of blood mingled with fish slime against my tongue. I wanted to gag. Grandfather retrieved my half-cleaned fish and rinsed it in the bucket. He finished gutting the fish. One cut along the belly and innards flicked out with bare hands. "If your knife is sharp, you must be controlled in your movements," he said. "That is the other thing to remember." I sat on the floor of the boat, thumb in mouth, and nodded.

My finger throbbed and I longed to go home, but dared not mention discomfort. Satisfied I wasn't seriously hurt, Grandfather ignored me and continued to fish. The cormorants swarmed him, their throats distended, and clamoured for attention. He turned and drew each onto the deck one at a time, removed their fish, and sent them back to the river. Clipped wings beat against the surface of the water and disrupted the night sounds, masked the crickets' song. Around and around the boat they circled, like the sky that swirled above our heads. Like constellations pivoting on a fixed point.

Grandfather was not a man to talk, but during the years I fished with him, he taught many things. Practical knowledge he gave by example and expected me to absorb through observation: How to handle the cormorants and how to bargain for the best price at the markets. How to propel the boat in a straight line and how to perform basic maintenance and upkeep. Useful information for a time we both knew would come, a time when he would be gone.

Sometimes though, when the night was particularly slow, or he felt urged by the changing seasons, he told stories. Stories of my great-grandfather's grandfather and the ancient emperors. Stories from before. He pointed at the sky with lined, callused hands and showed the Milky Way—not simply a far-flung arm of our galaxy, but the celestial river that separates the Weaving Maiden from her Cowherd. It glimmered from the distance as I floated on my own river. Another time, when the autumn moon shone brightest and coldest, he spoke of Jade Rabbit. With mortar and pestle, the rabbit grinds the elixir of immortality for the Moon Goddess Chang'e. My naked eyes searched the craters of the moon and I traced the outline of long ears on the glowing surface. Maybe I imagined. One night, as he gutted an especially beautiful fish, he told me how long long ago, a carp triumphantly swam up a great waterfall and leaped over the Dragon's Gate. Grandfather re-enacted the scene with the fish in his hand. I didn't even notice him moving the fish, invisible and hidden in the background. I saw only the carp, not dead, but resurrected and glorious, pushing against the current of the Yellow River. Because of his strength and bravery, the fish was transformed into a dragon. A scaly and powerful one, long-whiskered and yellow-bellied, equally at home in the water and the sky. Grandfather told these stories with a low cracking voice and animated eyes. Stories of magical times that were slipping away, slowly obscured by the dust of a changing world.

My nights ended when we returned from the river, but Grandfather's did not. Each night, after I lay on the mat next to Older Sister, he left the hut a second time and went to the places where some men are made and some are lost. In the mornings Grandfather came home early from the mah-jong halls and would skulk in with red eyes and greasy hair. The smell of cheap rice wine emanated from his clothes and his mouth, even from the pores of his skin. Sometimes he won, more often not, so he brought his debt home as well. The losses and gains fluctuated, but we absorbed the expense and the pattern continued until one morning, when I was twelve and Grandfather did not return until long after the sun had risen. When he finally came home, he would not meet my mother's eyes and crumpled into bed like a dried-out spider.

Thus began the day my mother drank cup after cup of weak tea. She sat at the wooden table still as a stone lion. I waited for her eyes to drip blood like the guardian lions in the flood stories, but not even water fell. She stared straight ahead, square face framed by dark black hair, and waited for the liquid to cool. When it was tepid, she downed it and poured another. She didn't move for six hours. Not to work in the rice paddies, not when the sun sank below the horizon and I lit the lamps. Not even when my baby sister pulled on her loose clothes and complained of hunger. Older Sister finally boiled plain congee and fed it to the baby. We put a bowl in front of my mother, but she didn't eat. Older Sister and I shared the rest of the runny porridge straight from the pot. Grandfather slept on.

Finally, when the night had fully fallen, Mother roused herself from the table. She lit our last three sticks of incense and stabbed them into a pot of sand. Sicksweet. With a burnished key, she unlocked the wooden box that sat by her bed and pulled off the yellow silk liner. The three coins glittered and flashed when she placed them on the table. I'd seen her consult the I Ching many times before this, but never with such ceremony. She passed the coins around for each person to warm. The tip of my smallest finger barely fit through the square hole in the centre. I was unable to generate any heat, the coins remained cold in my hands. I gave them to Older Sister; she squeezed tightly and breathed into her palms. Even baby sister had to do it. Older Sister helped her, she held the baby's fat hands around the shiny coins and chanted rhymes to distract her. Satisfied we'd prepared properly, Mother threw those coins on the table six times. Metal clanged on wood and she jerked her hand and sent them skittering across the table.

She radiated controlled violence, completely focused on her task. My hands began to shake. I was often afraid of my mother, of her strength and her fury, but never as much as then. She marked the results on rough paper and studied them for some time. Silence followed, and it settled in my ears.

When she'd left the table, I looked at what my mother had written. Older Sister stood beside me and we pored over the calligraphy. My head reached her shoulder. On the bottom, three open lines—Li, the clinging, fire. On top, two open lines and one closed—Ken, keeping still, mountain. Together they formed the hexagram Po, the splitting apart. Older Sister ran her hands through her hair, longer than Mother's and perhaps even finer. Supposedly, she had inherited our father's looks. Small bones, delicate facial structure. "Do you know what that one means," she asked. I nodded. Splitting apart, deterioration. I knew as well as she did, nothing could be done.

Mother didn't let Grandfather touch the money we gathered. Instead, she made me walk with her to the darkest part of the village, where I never ventured. We entered the gambling hall together. Tables were scattered around the dim room, gas-lit, and smoky. Red and gold good luck scrolls hung from the walls, their edges curled. They promised good fortune, prosperity, auspicious beginnings. And they could be had by every gambler, if only they were bold enough, clever enough. If only they had another chance. Men and women, young and old, crowded around grimy tables to watch the games. Watch the click-clack of the white tiles stacked into low walls, the faces emotionless and concentrated, slight frowns. The calculation of risk. I could not picture my grandfather in this place, yet the smell that clung to his clothes when he returned each night was the same. The only familiarity in a hall of new sights.

Mother asked a boy for Mr. Wang and we were told to wait while he fetched him. We did not have to stand for long. Mr. Wang strode toward us before I could ask Mother any of the questions that swam through my water-filled head. His frame was big and covered by a blue silk robe embroidered with scenes of the ocean. His bald head sweated freely. Mother handed him a purse. He sniffed, inspected the contents, and peered at us.

"The rest will be here soon," my mother assured him.

He grunted. "The old man gets his daughter to pay his debts?"

"He wished to come himself, unfortunately he has new birds to train," my mother answered evenly.

"Or he's ashamed to show his face."

My mother did not respond. She turned to me. "We'd better go, much to do at home."

We left the smelly hall and I was glad to breathe fresh air. Soon the grungy buildings gave way to the wooden shacks of the villagers, worn but still maintained. Chickens ran freely and pecked the ground for stray grains. Pebbles from the dirt road poked my bare feet and I winced but Mother kept her pace. Halfway home, at the riverbank, she stopped and turned to me, her thick eyebrows raised and mouth contorted. "Son, you must never gamble," she said. "It will be years before we are free of this." She grabbed my earlobe and yanked downward. "Do you understand?" Pain blossomed and I nodded. Her face softened, and she traced my cheek with a rough finger. She began to walk again and I followed, careful not to fall behind.

—

That night we did not fish. Grandfather had not risen from bed. We ate quickly, steamed vegetables and rice. Mother did not save any for Grandfather. We unrolled our sleeping mats and spread out. Eager for the extra rest, I fell asleep immediately.

In the middle of the night I awoke to a noise. My grandfather had stumbled out of bed. I rolled on my side to get a better view over Older Sister. Grandfather dressed quickly. First, he slipped on his old shirt and struggled with the knotted buttons. Next, soft pants, still stained and now crumpled as well, pulled over bony legs and caught on his knees. He rolled the sleeves of his shirt to his elbows and his pant legs halfway up his calves. Last night's clothes. His breath wheezed in his chest and his silhouette bent even more than before. I couldn't believe he would gamble again, after all that had happened, but the call had not left his blood. He paused at the door and looked at me. I'm sure he could sense I was awake. I froze, squeezed my eyes shut. To my relief he did not speak before he left.

That was the last time I saw him. He did not return to the mah-jong halls. Grandfather's body was found the next morning on the riverbank, two villages downstream.

Mother did not seem surprised that Grandfather was dead. She did not drink endless cups of tea although I boiled water for her. She did not consult the I Ching. The oracle had spoken and she had already grieved her loss. Instead, she cooked northern dumplings with pork. We rarely ate meat and the richness wormed uneasily in my stomach. The baby ate noisily and pulled the dough apart with fat hands. Older Sister stabbed her food and ate only one of the white half moons piled in her bowl. Pale-faced, she gave the others to me. I wasn't hungry either, but ate so she wouldn't have to. "Son, you must fish tomorrow night," Mother said after she'd finished her last dumpling. "And I will buy more fertilizer."

For three years, I would fish at night as my grandfather had done. At first the cormorants were suspicious, I had rarely been allowed to handle them. In the beginning I spent much time by their bamboo cages, offered morsels of fish, and cooed gently. I didn't like to think of Grandfather, but I found myself mimicking his actions, the way he had interacted with the birds. In time, they came to trust me and my catch became quite good. Never plentiful as when I worked with Grandfather. I was unable to handle the same number of birds as him and still manage the boat. But for a while we survived this way.

Six months after Grandfather died, Older Sister left our home to marry a man from the north. We didn't hear from her after she left. Mother said she must be too busy running a household to write. She didn't tell me about the small pile of money she received from the well-dressed man who would escort Older Sister to her new home, but I saw the exchange through the open door when I came home one night. I didn't see her take the money to Mr. Wang either, but I knew the smell of the gambling halls well enough to guess where the money had gone. I cursed Grandfather.

Of course, there came a time when even combined with my mother's work in the fields, the fishing was no longer enough. I wasn't catching as much as before and increased competition with newer fishing technology lowered market prices for carp. China was on the rise, and tradition was left behind in favour of efficiency.

Mother decided the thing to do was sell. She and baby sister would move to Hong Kong and work in the factories. She knew a woman who moved from the village to work in a leather purse factory and thought she could get a job. A real city job, one that paid well. I thought I would go with her, but Mother had other plans. I would use the bulk of whatever money remained to go to Canada. In the new lands, the lands filled with promise and possibility, I would find fortune. When I had made enough I would sponsor her and baby sister and we would live in Vancouver—the city by the sea. She wanted to open a restaurant. I sold my boat and my birds and prepared to travel.

Although most Chinese immigrants in British Columbia worked in the canneries after the railroad was finished, I had a good boat sense and was willing to put myself deeper in debt to live off the sea. For a few seasons, I trolled at Cape Mudge on the Gulf of Georgia. At the time it was the most popular area for hand trolling. This was in part because of the established shacks for fishermen to live in and in part because of the fish. For me, and I can say this with certainty now, those early years were the strangest time of my life. The time when I couldn't decide if I was homesick or excited, Chinese or Canadian, child or man. The boundary years, I call them, on the West Coast.

One morning, near the end of my first season, I took my boat as usual and prepared to fish. The day was going to be hot, I could tell by the sky. The skidway was busy and cramped. Some men joked and helped each other pull their skiffs into the water. I preferred to work alone and most men preferred not to talk to me. Luckily, the only rowboat I could afford was small enough to manage. An eight-foot tubby weathered grey from the salt. It didn't leak, but a small amount of scummy water in the bottom resisted the bailer. I dropped my gear in—line, extra hooks, knife—and my body cramped in anticipation of another full day.

I rowed into the sound, and the landscape and its newness assaulted me from each direction. Salt and the dark trees. Cold wind from the sea mixed with damp forest smells to create a scent I could not adjust to. I longed for sicksweet incense. The sea rolled beneath me, wave under wave. This water was alive. I gripped the oars and pulled. Unlike on the river, I had to decide my own course. Bright white seagulls screamed and fought on the rocky shore. One found a dead crab and the others swarmed. He squawked and rushed to defend his food. I disliked seagulls and their pointed yellow beaks. Nasty, violent birds.

I let out my line and baited my hooks with a bit of herring from the day before. After securing the tackle to the boat, I dropped the whole thing overboard and gently rowed. I was new to ocean fishing, but the past months had taught me to find the right currents. The bait had to look natural in the water or the salmon wouldn't take it. Their intelligence had to be respected. The key to success, I eventually found, was to understand that it was not fishing, rather, something much closer to seduction. The hand troller's job was to determine the preferences of the fish, to adjust their practice accordingly, and to coax the fickle salmon to strike. At that time, still relatively unskilled, I used a single trolling line as opposed to the herring rake other fishermen used to spear multiple fish at once.

I caught a few small bluebacks with clear eyes, but nothing of great value. Time for a new spot. I picked up the oars and enjoyed the sound of creaking in the oarlocks, the strain in my arms. At a small kelp bed, I re-baited with renewed enthusiasm. My movement disturbed an otter and it dived underwater. I took this to be a good sign. My legs cramped and the ache diffused through my body. I wished to stand and stretch but feared the boat would tip. Instead, I flexed each muscle in isolation. Toes, feet, calves. All at once, a promising tug on the line. I pulled, but the hook had only snagged on a bit of seaweed, slimy and dark. Nothing for me.

The day drew on and I became more hot and irritable. I wished for a hat but didn't have one. My stomach growled but I hadn't brought food. The sun glared on the sea and lulled me into lethargy. The trees on the shoreline blurred into a hazy smudge. I caught a few more small fish, and then a decent-sized Coho. Dense for its length, firm-fleshed with a cavernous mouth and oddly thick lips.

Now listen. You, with your modern ideas, might not believe this part, but it's true. That fish looked like a person. It gaped at me and sputtered and thrashed as I took it off the line. Calculated eyes stared with an arrogance ordinary creatures do not possess.

"Li Shen," it said my name.

I jumped. Partially in surprise and partially because it had been so long since I'd heard my name aloud. I blinked and looked back and forth to the horizon, but the fish had certainly spoken for there was nothing else but the sea.

"Do you know me?" it asked.

I looked closer. The silver scales flashed a deep blue and the air smelled thick. For a moment I couldn't place it. Thick air. Blue scales. "Mr. Wang."

He grinned.

"My family has come to ruin because of you." I shook the fish in my hand and shouted.

"I made my living honestly," he said. "After your grandfather's death, I did not even charge your mother interest on the remainder of the debt." He gestured toward me, thick fin extended. "You are a bad luck family. Nothing can change that." He struggled, gasped, and went limp.

Mr. Wang lay still in my hand. I shook him again, but the essence of the man had left with the death of his body. His eyes continued to stare at me. Dull. His slime oozed onto my skin and the smell of the gambling parlour lingered in the air, barely perceptible under the smell of the sea. The wind had picked up, and the water's surface crinkled like a fine blue silk robe. The shoreline appeared distant, far away, and out of reach. I floated in my boat and searched for something, anything to grasp on to. Only the sound of my breath. Rapid at first, but steadier the longer I sat.

Though thoroughly unsettled, I didn't see any point in wasting good fish. I washed Mr. Wang and put him in the bottom of my boat with the rest of my catch. Despite placing him under the other fish, his presence was undeniable, like a family ghost. In an effort to ignore him, I re-baited the line and waited. A good hour passed before I got another bite. This fish was easy to pull. It didn't have much fight. I knew who it was before I pulled it out of the water.

"Older Sister," I said. "What did we do to you?"

The fish smiled at me. "Little Brother, you have grown so big."

"Why did you never write to us?"

"I wished to, but I never had the chance." She spoke without emotion. She was worn out. Sickly. Her fins nearly translucent and gills pale. I unhooked her quickly and held her in the water. She did not struggle in my hand but rested there. Her scales cool and smooth against my palm.

"Was your husband good to you, Older Sister?" I asked.

"Brother, there was no husband. I went with a man named Mr. Fa and we travelled to Hong Kong. I was sold to a brothel and I worked for three years. I will not speak of the shame I endured, but I became sick and I did not live long. Now I swim with the fish and the dragons beneath the water. I hoped to see you, brother." Her mouth barely moved when she spoke, still I understood.

"Mr. Fa lied to us."

"I'm sure our Mother knew. Do not blame her, she had no choice."

The fish looked at me and though I could clearly see the scales and the fins, the spirit of my sister shone through. I saw her in the gleam of her eyes, the grace of her movements. "Don't be sad for me, Little Brother. Now I am free to travel the world. There is a whole kingdom for me here. I have companions and I can do as I please. In a few years I will travel upstream to spawn and then I will die again. I may be reborn as a spirit of the wind or maybe one of your cormorants."

I tried to organize my thoughts to respond, but Older Sister was already leaving. Her tail pushed against my palm, surprisingly strong.

"Goodbye, Little Brother." She slipped out of my fingers, away from my grasping hands, and dived deep.

Yet again, I was alone on the water. In ancient times, spirits often came to speak with humans, but I had not realized they would follow me to the new world. So much I hadn't realized. I rowed away from that place without attention to direction. I had to move, to channel my thoughts. My arms ached and sweat dribbled across my forehead. The sun beat on. Gulls screamed on the shore but when I looked at them, I saw big black birds with fish in their throats.

My day's catch: four small fish and Mr. Wang. I was tempted to row back to shore and get off that strange ocean, but I knew I needed to do better. I had nowhere near the amount of money required to sponsor my mother and sister. The sun was still high, but it had begun to slip. Not much time left. I waited and waited and waited. I sat for hours, a statue, but nothing bit. The landscape moved around me but the boat and I remained immobile. About to give up and go home, I finally got a bite.

It was going to be bigger than the others. Maybe a big Coho. I pulled evenly, careful not to thrash. I didn't want to blemish the flesh. The canneries paid better for perfect fish. That's why they bought their high-grade stock from hand trollers, who caught each individually.

My day with the spirits was not over. Grandfather, no longer bent and weak but a strong fish, shone with bright silver scales and piercing eyes. I almost dropped him back into the water. Seeing Mr. Wang and Older Sister was one thing, but Grandfather.

"I've missed you, Grandson." His voice brought it back. The birds, the river, years of fishing. Years I yearned to live again. Years in the past. I tried to pull the hook from his mouth, but the barb stuck fast in his lip. I yanked and ripped the skin.

"Forgive me," he said.

I'm still not sure what took hold of me in that moment, but it was terrible. I grabbed him in my arms and he began to thrash. I smashed him on the side of the rowboat. The gulls floating nearby scattered at my screams. I must've looked like a mad man alone in my boat. Again and again I hit him. I hit for every cup of tea my mother drank. I hit him for every coin we threw. I hit him for Older Sister. For every white man who called me a chink or slanty-eyes or said to me, "Hey, you know how the Chinamen name their babies? Drop a spoon on the floor and see what sound it makes—Ching, Chang, Chong." I hit until my strength was gone. He was long dead by the time I stopped. The flesh that would have brought so much money was pocked and damaged.

Control is the most important thing. After it was over, I breathed hard and sat with Grandfather in my lap. The eyes were dull. I knew exactly what I had to do. I rinsed him in salt water and pulled out my knife. One clean cut from under his chin to the tail. I applied the perfect amount of pressure. Splitting apart. His insides oozed and I reached in and pulled them out. I threw the snarl overboard and the seagulls shrieked and descended. They pulled and fought over his intestines. For a while their noise was overwhelming, but the racket hushed as I rowed home.

You. You walked in here wearing your yellow sweater with a tin of lemon squares in one hand and yesterday's *Globe and Mail* under your arm. Together we ate the bars dusted with icing sugar, two each. Now fine crumbs cover my blankets and I will feel them scratch at my back when I sleep. You're bold, but your small hands still curl around the bedcovers when you ask questions. In your face, I recognize many you will never know, spirits now. I see your great-aunt's fine long hair, your great-grandmother's strength. You should be in school, but you are here. Your mother will be angry.

The facts are these: In 1905, I was born in a small village on the banks of the Xi River in Guandxi Province. My mother worked in the rice paddies. My father died when I was very small. Five of us lived in a one-room shack by the river. Mother, Grandfather, Older Sister, the baby, and me. We were poor, but so was everyone. We managed. At fifteen, I came to Canada and fished on the West Coast. I worked hard on the ocean and came to know it. You might call me successful. I never saw my family again.

So, now you know, little swallow. Not everything, enough. Soon I will be one of those people who drinks thickened orange juice with a spoon. I have seen trays of these in the dining room, lined up like glasses of Jell-O. At least I'm on the ground floor, where bingo night is every Thursday and we're allowed walks. Still, we must be realistic; my time is limited. I feel weaker every day. But you, you know the story of the day the fish spoke. It's yours to keep or yours to tell. Like the call of a brass gong, each of your words rings clear. And the sound you make echoes into the distance, beyond everything I know.

FRANCESCA EKWUYASI

ỌRUN IS HEAVEN

Part One

You come from a heap of floating logs on the sea and worn wooden houses swaying on stilts to the rhythm of the ocean breeze. And many many decrepit canoes; handmade with a fervour borne of passionate need. You come from a need so profound it feeds on itself, embellishes its acute lack with an urgent ingenuity. A more forgiving place would call it innovation, but you know it's a simple matter of survival. You come from a place whose inherent endurance seeps inside your skin and teaches you that nothing is so barren, so painful, so desperate, that it cannot be made bearable, even beautiful, even fruitful.

The heap of logs from which you come is tied together with ropes woven from plastic bottles that have been flattened, stretched thin and pliable. The logs amass and sprawl out, biting chunks out of the fetid lagoon to become quite a magnificent slum.

You come from a gorgeously magnificent slum, its name is Jagajaga, and you love it ferociously.

You love that your home has legs; the house that your mother built with discarded slabs of termite-ridden teak wood and mahogany stands on thin legs in deep water. And it reminds you with every groan, bend, and sway that you are lucky to be alive. Lucky, because despite how you tempt fate by existing in that house, in that slum, you and your people are yet to be swallowed up by the filthy water. Instead, the water feeds and yields to you. It cradles you. The water has marked you and your people; a deep blue and webby constellation of veiny lines climbs your feet, all the way up your legs and torso, arms and neck, delicate cursive lines snake around your faces. They make an intricate map of your body and adorn your skin so that one look and it is clear that you are slum water people. It started in your grandmother's grandmother's generation. They thought it was a disease, grotesque, tried to pray it away and ate fistfuls of white medicine, but it persisted. Now your people understand: it's just Sişa, the water's mark that makes it so that you cannot drown, and no matter what else lives inside of it, the water will never poison you.

You are in your neighbour's canoe with your sister, Lailai. You've tied the boat to a crooked leg of the house that you share, and it rocks you both gently in a soothing cadence. You tilt your face up to the inky sky, and you unburden your mind.

You say, "Walahi, I'm exhausted!"

And you are. The feat to make ends meet is exhausting. Tonight, for example, you will work a shift at Sun Bukkah. You will dance on the crooked and scuffed mirror stage for measly tips, and you will massage the backs, shoulders, and groins of new and regular, often handsy, customers for a bit more. Tomorrow morning you will hope that the gum patch on your canoe has adequately sealed as you paddle to the Jagajaga community school, where you will teach the children of last night's customers basic math and spelling. Afterwards, you will care for the infants at the House of Yemaya, so that their mothers can worship and commiserate without the constant interruption of wailing babies. For this, you will get paid in food that will last half the week, maybe a day more if you are frugal about portion sizes: cooked rice, peppery vegetable stew, smoked catfish. And prayers, which will last however long blessings are said to live on through the ears of the creator.

You tell your sister, "I'm considering going to Ọrun. I can find better work there, send you money so you can rest, come back every few months . . ."

Lailai's thick eyebrows make a tight knot; she shakes her head and flicks her thumb in an outward motion on the bottom of her chin: "Don't."

She doesn't speak with words, never has. In all her eighteen years no voice has grown in her throat, so with swift hands, she signs, "Nobody comes back from Ọrun, don't leave me here."

You reach for her hands, but she moves away from you, rocks the boat precariously with her sudden jerking movement. Salty tears come quickly; they fill her large eyes; she is crying convulsively because she can see that you've already decided.

Lailai is wrong; people do come back from Ọrun, or more truthfully, one person has recently come back from Ọrun. Paradise, a childhood friend who left with Labour Recruiters six years ago, showed up earlier in the week at the primary school where you teach. She'd waited until you sent the children home before stepping into the classroom.

You didn't recognize her at first glance; you thought she was one of those misguided and insufferable aid workers because her skin was plain, blank, no Siṣa curled and dotted down her bare arms or peeked over the high neckline of her stiff and impeccably clean kaftan. But you recognized the song of her voice when she spoke your name. "Ife!" she exclaimed. "Long time!"

"Paradise?" you'd asked, eyes narrowed. "Kai! Long time! What are you doing here?"

"I'm looking for you now!"

"You look . . ." You'd shaken your head, nearly at a loss for words. "Well, you look very well. What happened to your skin?" You gestured to the plainness of her lean arms.

"I'll gist you later, but you, you still teach here?" Her question was punctuated with a high note that you registered as pity.

"I do." You nodded and swallowed a scoff.

"And you're still at Sun Bukkah?"

"I am." You nodded again, wringing the damp rag in your hands.

"And dredging?" Her tone grew more incredulous with each question; her eyes widened as if in disbelief. She grew up in Jagajaga, she knew how it was.

Shame crept up the back of your neck, but you kept a placid smile, shrugged, and said, "When there's demand, yes, whenever I can."

"Oh girl, you never tire?!" She sat cross-legged on the desk directly across from you, the fabric of her tight trousers shone like sleek black oil.

You recalled the year Paradise left, the same year your mother vanished without a word, the same year you started to dance at Sun Bukkah to keep Lailai from hunger while you both mourned your mother's absence. It would have been too much. It was still too much.

You surrendered, relaxed your jaw, your shoulders, looked your old friend in the face, and told the truth: "I don tire."

<hr />

Now you tell Lailai what Paradise told you:

Ǫrun is heaven, the water is sweet, the work is plenty, and they pay well. And nobody can vanish there. Camera eyes everywhere and it is safe. But Lailai remains unconvinced. She shakes her head and signs, "Nobody comes back from Ǫrun."

You will leave in two days, but in those two days, you will work more than you will not, so you say your goodbyes now.

For a long time you cling to each other in a tight and tearful and painful embrace, then Lailai pulls away and signs, "Don't forget that Ife is Love."

You attempt to memorize the details of her face awash in cool and electric moonlight, the way that her Sìsà underlines her right eye with a thin outward-curving line, the thick twisted locs framing her face with a blunt fringe, her broad nose, and cheeks still round with puppy fat late into her teenage years. You say, "I won't forget that Lailai is Forever. I will come back."

The motorboat that takes you from Jagajaga to Ọrun has the word *Shakara* written in red across its shiny white body. It is small, but it moves like new. You don't believe you've seen a new object since you were small. Even the donated screens at the school first passed through the soft hands of mainland children before they got to your students. This boat is new, its solar panels are intact, almost pristine, and it moves swiftly through the water that gets clearer and bluer the closer it takes you to Ọrun.

There are six of you on *Shakara*. Two Labour Recruiters, identical thickset mainland men with plain skin, introduce themselves as Uche and Caleb. They are sitting with the boat captain. Paradise is sitting between you and Chichi Girl, one of the mothers from the House of Yemaya. Chichi Girl is crying silently; she is leaving her ten-month-old, Oyin. Oyin's name is fitting. Like her mother, her skin is the colour of dark honey; their Sịṣa is almost identical. You reach a hand across Paradise to hold Chichi Girl's hand. You say, "My sister, e pẹlẹ. She will be there when you get back."

She turns to look at you, but it's too raw, the anguish in her eyes, so you avert your own. You look at your hand on her hand and squeeze.

Paradise shifts in her seat with impatience or annoyance, you're not sure, so you release Chichi Girl's hand and ask, "Paradise, how long between home and Ọrun?"

"Abeg, that place is not my home. No dey ask me long question." She doesn't look at you. Her features are stoic. All the warm familiarity of a few days ago has melted away to reveal a cold indifference. Taken aback, you roll your neck, raise your eyebrows, and blink slowly for effect.

"Na me you dey follow talk like that? Because I dey ask simple question? Na wa o!" You suck your teeth and look away.

⸺⸙⸺

Chichi Girl has stopped crying. She is staring ahead, blank-faced, resolved. You try to mimic her demeanour even though by now you worry that the work arrangement promised by Paradise and the Labour Recruiters will not be quite as they described. One of the Recruiters, you're not sure which one, gestures for you to stretch out your arm, and when you hesitate he grabs it with less force than you expected. He circles a thin silver hoop around your wrist. He does the same to Chichi Girl.

Turning back to look at you, he says, "ID bracelet. They will scan it at the Port." He points a thick finger inches from your nose. "You are Aminata."

He turns to Chichi Girl and says, "You are Caro."

Next, Paradise joins you. She opens a slim metal case, small enough to fit in her slender palm. Without looking at you, she says, "I have to put these lenses in your eyes. The same as the bracelet, it's for the biometric eye scan; it has all of Aminata's information. Don't rub your eyes or they will suspect."

You see it long before the boat docks. Ọrun is sprawling splendour, sparkling buildings clawing at the sky with their spires of polished metal and glass. You wonder how they keep it so clean; for many miles, before you reach it, the water is clear. No plastic bags, no plastic bottles, no tangled mass of filthy garbage. Instead, only bright pink buoys dot the sea, large balls with undersides encrusted in tiny dark molluscs, swaying up and down in the calm waves that grow more restless with the boat's arrival. You get close enough to one of the buoys just as a seagull swoops down to peck at it. Even the bird is unnaturally clean. Fastened to its left leg, just above its webbed feet, you see a thin strap with a blue oval half the size of the nail on your little finger. In the oval, a blinking orange dot. An identical oval is blinking on top of the buoy. Eyes. You heard about the eyes everywhere. You didn't expect to see them from this far out. You turn your face away on instinct.

⁓

Paradise and the Labour Recruiters are waiting outside by a white van with the words *Gaskiya Inc.* written across the door in green cursive lettering. You and Chichi Girl enter the back of the van after Paradise, with the Labour Recruiters hulking behind you.

Seated beside Paradise, you ask without looking at her, "Who is Aminata?"

"She is a sim," she responds with aloofness. "She doesn't exist. Madame has her hackers create sims to transport workers. For now, you are Aminata." She scratches her elbows and looks around the van in agitation. "But we can deactivate the sim whenever we want, and then you will be no one."

Still scratching, she looks through the front window as the van begins to weave its way through the impeccably paved streets of downtown Ọrun. The traffic rushes forward, and bright people in their colourful clothes and shiny bicycles populate the sidewalk. You speed by dazzling storefronts and massive screens advertising facial reconstruction sessions, virtual reality fitness plans, new television series, the jackpot lotto—currently at fifty-six million Ọrun Nairas—Gaskiya teas and spices, fair trade, organic, ethically sourced, fair labour certified, and Ringer Networking.

"Madame?" Chichi Girl asks, panic rising in her voice with each word. "Who is Madame? You said we could stay with you until we find work."

Laughter erupts from the driver's seat. From the rear-view mirror, you see bloodshot eyes, familiar crinkles at the corner.

"Paradise, you need to come up with better lies." You recognize the voice and lean forward for a closer look. You know the driver—Brother Fatai.

Brother Fatai is from Jagajaga. You haven't seen him in at least three years. A single father, his daughter, Kele, was one of your students. She was eager, sharp, funny; vanished when she was eleven years old. Vanished like your mother, like so many others back home. No explanation, no word, no body. The absence of a corpse makes the mourning that much more painful. Brother Fatai became a crumbling building, rotting and collapsing from the inside. His light dimmed and dimmed. The community rallied, brought him food, cleaned his place, donated money for his rent, never stopped searching for Kele. When he left with Labour Recruiters eight months after her disappearance, the community sighed in collective relief; he needed the change.

Now he is here, and you are here.

You want to announce yourself, but you bite your tongue and bide your time.

"Who is Madame?" Chichi Girl asks again.

"You will meet her shortly," Brother Fatai says. "Welcome to Ọrun. Paradise told you it's heaven, abi?" He chuckles, and it sounds like a cough. "You will soon find out for yourself."

⚬⚬⚬⚬

Genevieve Fath Korede, better known by her employees as Madame, is a deputy minister in the Ọrun Municipality Department of Labour. She is a senior board member of the Ọrun Ethical Work Association, the CEO of Gaskiya Inc., and, you learn, a key player in an extensive human trafficking network. She's a well-honed businessperson, and nothing turns a profit like free labour. A small woman, fine-boned and elegant, she glows with wellness as she sits within the folds of her vintage silk kimono.

"Welcome, my friends!" She beckons you and Chichi Girl into her office. You walk in, followed by Paradise and the Labour Recruiters.

Madame scans you both with shiny eyes. "Do you like the identities I rented for you?" Her petite hands gesture for you both to fill the two empty seats across from her.

"Rented?" Chichi Girl asks; this elicits a commiserate *Mhmm* from Madame.

"Aww, you slumling," she coos, "nothing in Ọrun is free, sweetie. I rented you those identities; you know, biometric contacts aren't cheap."

She cocks her head to the side and asks the Labour Recruiters, "Are they cheap, my boys?"

"No, Madame," Caleb and Uche reply in unison from behind you. Out of eyeshot their monotone voices are indistinguishable; one of them snickers, but you cannot tell which one of them is laughing at your plight. You decide to hate them both equally.

Chichi Girl turns to you, her features scattered in bafflement. "Ko ye mi." She doesn't understand.

You reach for her hand, and through gritted teeth, you say, "Paradise lied to us. When she told us that we could stay with her until we find work here, she lied."

You keep your eyes on her face and choke back any trace of the tears that are struggling to pour out of you. "What this woman, this Madame, is saying is that we owe her for this." You shake the silver bracelet on your wrist. "And for the transportation from Jagajaga to this place."

Still speaking to Chichi Girl, you turn to face Madame. "What she hasn't said yet is that she will deactivate our identity bracelets and report us to the Authorities if we don't do whatever she asks."

"I told you she was sharp," Paradise says from behind you; her tone is solemn, almost sorry.

"Sharp indeed." Madame arranges her features into a shape that would convey sorrow if you didn't know better. She offers, "I'm a benevolent employer; I will give you many options."

These are your options: You can borrow from her supply of paint to cover up your Sìṣà and, using your identities as Aminata and Caro, you can work as housekeepers or cleaners in any of the corporate buildings to which Madame supplies workers. You can work in the Pleasure Parlour, dance or fuck for money. If you don't want to borrow paint, you can only work in the Fetish section of the Pleasure Parlour. You can work as tea pickers on the Gaskiya Inc. tea plantation; you will live on the plantation if you choose this because the commute is much too long to expect Brother Fatai to drive you there and back every day. You can work washing dishes at one of the many fine dining restaurants in Ọrun. You won't need to cover up your Sịṣa for this, but you will earn considerably less if you choose not to. You can work as housegirls for an expat family—clean, cook, soothe fussy babies, never complain.

Whatever you choose, you must pay fifty per cent of your earnings for housing, twenty per cent for the paint to cover your Sịṣa, ten per cent toward your transportation, and another ten per cent for you identity bracelets. The remaining money is yours to keep for food and savings. However, if you eat from the kitchen, then you must pay five per cent of your earnings because, as Madame says, nothing is free in Ọrun.

⚬⚬⚬

The room you will share with Chichi Girl and eight other trafficked women is in the bowels of Madame's four-storey house. It is a stark and disheartening contrast to the opulence of the rest of the house. Five bunk beds line the walls of the dank room, and a solitary fan turns lazily, half-heartedly beating the thick air from where it hangs on the low ceiling.

Paradise shows you and Chichi Girl the empty bunk closest to the heavy entry door. Chichi Girl collapses on the bottom bed; stunned, she asks, "Paradise, you knew?"

"Abeg abeg, no dey ask me rubbish question," Paradise retorts with harshness.

Rage flares up inside you. You shove her against the door, and the sound that escapes your throat is loud and guttural.

You inhale, exhale, compose yourself, and with as much calmness as you can manage, you say, "You lied to us. Because of you, they've trapped us."

"It was you or me."

You shake your head and hiss with contempt: "They lied to you. If it's me, it's you; there's no 'or.'"

"She promised to clean my skin." She is crying suddenly. "Madame said if I get replacements, they will clean my skin and I won't have to be borrowing paint from her . . . I can save the money."

You ignore the pity that wants to sway you away from rage. You rebuff, "Paradise, are you foolish? Have you never been wounded? Sìṣà runs down to the bone. It cannot be 'cleaned.' There is nothing to 'clean.'"

"But Madame promised, she swore . . . I cannot live here with this Sìṣà. Even after I finish paying Madame, I won't be able to find work that pays well. I'm tired. Madame's paint makes me sick, and the good one is costly. My Sìṣà, the marks make my work cheap."

You shake your head and turn away from her, toward the bunk bed you will share with Chichi Girl. With your back to Paradise, you caution, "Your Sìṣà makes Jagajaga home, these people and this place make your work cheap. You should have stayed when you came to recruit me. We should have both stayed home."

<hr />

You are nearly asleep, close to the placid threshold of dreamless dark, when you are jerked awake by the creaking sound of the door opening, the muffled thud of a body landing on the stone floor, and the door slamming shut. You sit up from your perch on the top bunk that barely fits the length of your sore body. In the darkness you see a form rise from a pile on the floor; breathing heavy, a tall, lean familiar frame with locs swinging in thin curling tendrils down to their waist.

You ask in a hushed whisper, "Are you okay?"

"No," a tense voice replies, "no, I am not okay." They walk farther into the room, closer to your bunk, and you see outlines of features that you recognize.

"Ẹbun Mimọ?" you ask in utter disbelief.

She halts two feet away from you, gasping: "No."

Ẹbun Mimọ rushes to the side of your bunk and searches for your body with her slender hands. "Ife? No, go home."

"Ẹbun, my sister, what are you doing here?"

You find each other's hands and clutch tightly in the darkness. There is a long moment of heavy silence before Ẹbun Mimọ reveals, "I was working as a housegirl on the mainland, but the money was rubbish, I couldn't even save enough to go back to home once a month. When I found out what the other girls were making, I told my madam that I deserved an increase in wages, and she said she knows what kind of woman I am. She pointed to my lap and said that if I gave her any wahala, she would tell all the other mothers so no one would hire me."

"God punish her," you say. Sadness is taking concrete weight in your body now, wedged beside the exhaustion.

"I've petitioned Mama Yemaya to deal with her cruelty," Ẹbun Mimọ continues. "I heard that Ọrun was different, that I could live free, in peace, and work for money that makes sense."

In the darkness, you can smell the sharp scent of sweat from her body, mingled with the sweat and tears of the other sleeping women in the room, and moisture from the plumbing in the guts of the house.

"Maybe it is better here. Maybe they can see me clearly here like at home, but I don't know because these people won't let me go." She cries out. "It was humiliating; the madam upstairs made me strip down, she wanted to check the 'merchandise' as if I'm . . . I'm . . ."

Your grip on her hands tighten. "Then she told me I wasn't 'the kind of woman that they normally work with,' that I can work as a man or in a fetish club. Ife, I was on the path to becoming a priestess in the House of Yemaya. I cannot violate my oath for anything."

"I know," you say, "I know. I'm sorry, my sister. I'm so sorry for this." That is all you can say. It is all you can muster, as your own faith is fast depleting.

Ẹbun Mimọ asks about your sister, Lailai, and your heart breaks. You see Lailai's face before yours, bright as a new picture. When she turned thirteen, she shadowed Ẹbun Mimọ at the House of Yemeya, learning the rituals, offerings, and healing ceremonies.

Ẹbun Mimọ was vibrant and powerful, and she loved Jagajaga deeply. But even she, holy or not, exhausted with the constant hustle, chose to leave for better work. She eschewed the Labour Recruiters who routinely turn up and went to the mainland for familiar work. And yet, she still ended up here, in bondage with you.

Eight months. You do as Madame bids for eight bleak months, and you are not even nearly a quarter of the way to paying off your "debt." You are not surprised, but disheartened. And this disheartening plunges deeper than you knew possible; you are not in your body, and only barely in your mind. With Chichi Girl and Ẹbun Mimọ, you clean the bathrooms and service boudoirs at a fetish club near the Port called aGauche. At aGauche, you also shower for show; bathe in a glass-enclosed shower with cameras displaying you on screens throughout the club. It's for little extra pay, not as much as selling a fuck, but you've seen how the customers treat workers with Siṣa like yours. You've seen some of the femmes leave boudoirs with swollen eyes, chunks of hair missing from raw, weeping patches on their scalps, and worse. They walk out with empty faces, and that is what frightens you most.

None of you want to pay for paint to cover up your Siṣa because you can't bear to be further indebted to Madame, but also because you can see how it has burned harsh discoloured maps on Paradise's skin. When she scratches her arms, she comes away with peeled paint and bits of dead skin and gritty scabs underneath her fingernails. She hasn't spoken to you since your first evening here. She leaves the room in the morning with the rest of you, and Brother Fatai drops the lot of you at your respective work assignments and picks you up many hours later.

This evening you are waiting by the back entrance of aGauche, waiting for Brother Fatai to collect and drop you off at Platinum Plaza, the one-hundred-and-forty-five-floor office building in the condensed and dazzling centre of Ọrun. You are one of eighty-five workers, only a handful from Madame, who will clean cubicles, boardrooms, bathrooms, and staff break rooms until just before 3 a.m. when Brother Fatai will take you back to Madame's basement. You look around for Chichi Girl and Ẹbun Mimọ, who should be waiting with you, but there's no one else by the back entrance except for you and the many camera eyes scanning you, registering Aminata. This idea stirs up rage in you, but it is quickly dampened by worry; where are Chichi and Ẹbun?

Brother Fatai turns up in the white Gaskiya van, the door slides open smooth and near silent as usual. "The other girls aren't out yet," you say upon entering the vehicle.

"I know," Brother Fatai replies, pushing a button to slide the door shut. He hasn't directly looked at you since your first encounter at the Port months ago, hasn't acknowledged that you know each other from home. Now, alone in the van together, he keeps his eyes fixed on the road, and you do the same.

You ask, "Did you pick them up earlier? They came to work with me this morning . . ."

"Yes."

"Are they okay? We usually leave together."

This, he ignores.

You try again, prompting, "Did you take them back to Madame's house?"

He continues to drive in silence. When he pulls up to the north-facing door of Platinum Plaza, he lets you out of the van with a nod, his first gesture of acknowledgement. You step out, choking on your annoyance. You know that you are being scanned by the blue oval eyes planted throughout the building, the whole city; you want to return their gaze and scream until something shatters. Instead, you walk in with your head down and proceed to clean for six sluggish hours.

Back in Madame's basement, Chichi Girl and Ẹbun Mimọ
are absent from their hard creaky beds. You attempt to keep
your voice steady when you ask Paradise if she knows anything
about where they might be. And you tighten your fist to keep
from lashing out when she sucks her teeth, rolls her eyes, and
continues to pick at the sores on her arms. You don't sleep;
you rise at 7 a.m. with the rest of the workers to fill Brother
Fatai's van. Still no Chichi Girl or Ẹbun Mimọ.

At aGuache, in the din of the eternal pleasure that it sells,
you ask co-workers what they know. "Have you seen these
girls? They've been gone too long."

Most of them shake their heads impatiently, but one, Casha,
a cleaner like you, says, "Yesterday a customer wanted to buy
your friend, the tall one, but he—"

"She," you correct her.

She only shrugs. "Eh, yes, she said she doesn't sell fucks,
she just cleans. But the customer is a big man in Ọrun, plenty
of money, so Oga said that he—sorry, sorry, she—must go
with the customer."

Bile is rising in your stomach. Ẹbun Mimọ doesn't want to
do sex work; even in Jagajaga, she worked every possible gig,
but never Sun Bukkah.

"What happened?" You ask, clenching and releasing your
fist to move the tension that is mounting in your weary body.

"Ah, sister, it was bad o!" Casha lowers her voice and leans
closer to you. "Your friend fought the customer. Oga had to
send security inside—they called your people's agency, and
they came and collected her. It happened quick quick."

"And the other one, Chichi Girl?"

"The one who is always crying?"

"Yes."

"When Oga called your agency, he said they should take both of them because they are spoiling the show in his club."

You are going to break, you know it, you are going to break. You wheeze, struggle to inhale, to catch the air that is escaping you. You feel tears wet your cheeks just as your body begins to tremble.

"Sister," Casha says, "sister, I'm going to touch your shoulder now, okay?" She places a tentative hand on your bare shoulder; her hands are colder than you expected.

"Sister, look at me," she continues, "look at my face." Casha's face is the colour of milky tea, unmarked, she is not from your slum. Maybe a mainlander. Her eyelids are dusted with gold glitter, lips painted black, she is being kind to you. Her hand on your bare skin is reminding you that you have not been touched with tenderness in a long time. It evokes intense memories of your sister, Lailai.

"What is your name? Your name that your people call you?"

"Ife."

"Okay, Ife, stay focused. Remind yourself who you are. Worry about your friends when you leave. Oga is still very angry. Okay?"

You nod, Okay. You want to say thank you, but you are afraid you will cry if you open your mouth.

Alone in the van with Brother Fatai again. As soon as the door slides shut, you ask, "Where did they take them?"

He ignores your question.

You lunge forward, lodge your body into the space between the driver and passenger seat, and snatch the keys out of his dry callused hands. "Brother Fatai, what did they do to them?"

He is stunned by your outburst. He looks directly at you for the first time. He stares for a long moment before saying, "You remember me."

"Of course I do."

"I wasn't sure . . ."

"Please tell me, where are Chichi Girl and Ẹbun Mimọ? Are they alive, did Madame have you harm them?"

He shakes his head slowly and scoffs without joy: "A dead worker is not profitable."

You feel tears roll down your cheeks, your fist tightens around the jagged teeth of the car keys.

"She sent them to Gaskiya farm, to the tea plantation. She says it's the only place that they are profitable, they can cry and pray all they want, as long as they pick tea." He starts the engine and begins to drive.

"How can you do this to our people?"

"You know my Kele loved you?" he asks after a long pause. "I remember before they started donating screens to your school, you used to let her bring your screen home."

You remember too. Kele was often eager to get a head start on the next lessons, so you lent her your only screen to practise at home. She always remembered to bring it back, covered in greasy finger smudges but with the next day's lessons done, mostly correctly.

"She was one of the few who could do the work on her own," you say, softened by the memory.

"She loved you for it."

"I'm sorry."

"Me too."

He pulls up at the north-facing entrance of Platinum Plaza and turns off the engine. He takes his black hooded jacket off and throws it on the van floor beside you.

"Hood up, head down. Sister Circle, a blind shelter so no cameras, no questions. If you run now, you will be there before city sweep." He says this quickly, and in such a low tone you are not entirely sure if you're hearing correctly.

"The phone in the pocket," he continues, "emergencies only, nothing is analog."

You are frozen to the seat, stunned at what he is telling you until he shouts, "Go!"

You grab the jacket off the floor, throw the car keys at him, and dive out of the car, pulling it over your body as you stumble across the sidewalk, then you run. You run.

Part Two

Beside the wrought-iron gate of the shelter, there is a small indistinct sign that reads *Sister Circle*, with the word *Sister* crossed out and replaced with *Femme*. You are out of breath, wheezing as you walk into the building. A cathedral in its previous life, now its sacred halls are lined with narrow bunk beds, for the desperate and weary. Not unlike a church.

At the welcome desk sits a plain-skinned middle-aged woman with locs like Lailai's and a gold hoop encircling the septum of her large nose. She looks at you, smiles, and says, "Welcome."

You stare at her as you try to calm your breathing. You will your body to walk closer to the desk, you try to speak, but you only cry. Sniffling, hiccupping, coughing kind of cry.

She waits patiently, hands you a tissue, and hums soothing acknowledgements: "You're tired, aren't you? It's okay, take your time—take all the time you need."

When you stop crying, she looks at you and says, "My name is Sun. You don't have to tell me yours." You nod and attempt a feeble smile.

"Welcome to Femme Circle—or Sister Circle, whichever name works. The rules: no cameras, no weapons, no questions. I'm going to have to check you for weapons, pat you down old school. Do you consent?"

You nod your head, and it suddenly feels incredibly heavy. Sun pats you down, front and back, gentle pressure on parts of you where weapons could be hidden. Afterwards, she returns behind the desk and explains, "We operate on trust here, it's how we keep each other safe. If you'd like, we can pair you with a caseworker to help you through whatever it is that has brought you here. I can put you on a waitlist. Wait times are between five to seven months, better to sign up now, it might be up to a year by tomorrow morning."

You nod your head. Yes, you want a caseworker, although you cannot fathom how you will survive five to seven months without an identity. And Lailai—oh Lailai was right about Ọrun. Will you make it back to see her? Will you hug her and smell her tangerine smell again? Argue over cleaning the canoe again? These questions spins like a dust storm in your heavy head. It accompanies you to sleep after Sun has shown you to the bottom bed on a creaky bunk, with rows and rows of other occupied cots on either side of you, under a kaleido-scopic stained-glass ceiling.

———— ∞∞∞ ————

Six weeks at Femme Circle.

The first week you lived in a humid haze of sleep and weeping; you would wake from a dream of safety at home to find that you were still hiding in a decrepit cathedral, to find that your Chichi Girl and Ẹbun Mimọ were probably still working for nothing on Gaskiya tea plantation. It was all too crushing, so you went back to sleep, only to wake and face the same facts again each morning.

The second week Sun coaxed you out of bed to show you the dining hall, where a massive man with a tiny bleached-blond afro and marks flaring out from the corner of his lips served rice and beans, and bread and beans, and corn and beans, and beans and garri. You were ravenous and didn't grow tired of beans until week four. By then you had made some acquaintances, fellow inhabitants of the shelter. You shared laughs over nonsense. They were deep belly laughs that stole your breath. You laughed about fat rats, about the drip by the altar that could be Morse code, about the orchestra of flatulence that filled the rooms after dinners of beans.

You laughed into the fifth week, and you remembered your body. You hadn't looked at your body properly since you left Jagajaga; you used to watch your reflection when you danced in the mirrored walls of Sun Bukkah, sometimes with a slow hip-winding, a self-seduction that got you many tips.

You thought of your body most vividly when your bunk-mate, Zizzy, told you of her dating exploits on Ringer.

"I thought it was a networking app," you'd said as she climbed into the bed above you late at night.

"It's like a choose your own adventure for networking. You can set out to make professional contacts or personal contacts. I'm there for the personal evidently." Zizzy yawned and said, "You should check it out if you're keen."

"Is it safe?" you asked.

"I mean, you've got to be smart. If I'm looking to sell, then I demand we meet at a public place: a hotel or a club with rules. If it's just for fun, then I'm more flexible. But I always stay sober and never fall asleep."

Zizzy seemed like an open book, but there was a deep sadness, a dark well, just beneath her dazzling surface. You rose from your bed to face Zizzy, gestured to your Siṣa, and asked, "Zizzy, is it safe for me?"

Just then her bubbly surface receded and her sadness showed; she sighed and offered you a soft smile. "It's never safe for you here, baby girl, but give it a go; don't put up your face or geotag your location, but you already know that."

⸻

By now you have played out every ugly scenario that your mind can conjure. You have imagined it all; still, you fish out the sleek phone from the pocket of Brother Fatai's hooded jacket, you hold your thumb over the camera, and switch it on. Within seconds, you log in to the Ringer app that's already installed on the device.

You swipe across the screen. People have geotagged their location, the time, coordinates—they give away everything. You cannot connect until you create a profile, so you make one using the name Amen, and you take a picture from your breasts up to your chin. In the photo, your body jewels glint, the two on your nipples the brightest. Within two minutes of posting it without your location, you have twenty-three messages, most of them insults:

ugh clean skin only, this app has gone to shit

you people are everywhere

disgusting, scrub up

nice tits, but I don't fuck filthy slum sluts

shouldn't you be cleaning a toilet somewhere slum slut

Shame creeps up your neck but halts a moment when you read:

Your Sisa is gorgeous; I adore your embellishments.

You swipe to open the attached profile. It belongs to a woman, plain skin, her profile name Nirvana. You chuckle to yourself because it's absurd to claim to be a transcendent state, free of desire, while also trolling a free app for sex. But in the one picture on her profile, the woman has gorgeous lips and soft eyes, and you have a frantic longing to be touched. You reply.

It is gorgeous. But do your lips taste as good as they look?

Nirvana: *I'd like to think so, you want to find out?*

You: *yes*

Nirvana: *I'm at Affinity if you're keen on a night out*

You: *too many eyes*

Nirvana: *Camera shy?*

You: *yes*

Nirvana: *Soto is a blind club, meet there?*

You: *sure*

Nirvana: *I'll list you as my guest*

You do not join her at Soto; you cannot bring yourself to

leave the haven of Femme Circle because, despite your desires, you are terrified of being caught by the Authorities or by Madame's people. You don't know which situation would end worse for you. You are host to a goulash of contradicting impulses, but your sense of self-preservation prevails over horniness this evening.

Petrified for nearly two hours, after which you thaw and write a message.

Sorry can't make it out. Another time?

Nirvana: *For sure*

The stillness of the following morning is stirred by another message from Nirvana.

I assume you have a face?

You: *Who's to say?*

Nirvana: *That's intriguing*

You: *Is it now?*

Nirvana: *Do you have a whole torso?*

You: *Let me check . . . it appears that I do*

Nirvana: *That's very exciting*

You: 😄 *and you?*

Nirvana: *Oh I have a whole body, it's a pretty nifty thing to have these days.*

You: *What do you use it for?*

Nirvana: *Mostly for work, sometimes for dancing. You?*

You: *You're assuming I have a body . . . hehehe*

Nirvana: *Oh damn, I really hope you're a person, and I haven't been trying to flirt with a Bot*

You: *What if I'm a Bot who doesn't know she's a Bot?*

Nirvana: *That would be pretty sad, not that far off from what I do for work actually*

You: *What do you do for work?*
Nirvana: *I'm a programmer. Create code and whatnot*
You: *??*
Nirvana: *Hahaha! It's not terribly interesting*
You: *How do you know about Sìṣà?*
Nirvana: *Some friends from my previous job had the same*
You: *Coding job?*
Nirvana: *Yeah but for Open Borders, immigration justice stuff*
You: *Sounds noble*
Nirvana: *Is this very sexy conversation doing it for you?*
You: 😌 *yes*

And so it goes, through week seven and into week eight; your conversations with Nirvana feel like an anchor of normalcy. A kind of normalcy that isn't exactly normal to you, yet it feels good. And it feels good to feel good even if thoroughly coloured by guilt. So with a dab of red stain from Zizzy's callused finger; and your afro coaxed into braids that fall to the side of your face; and your rested body suited in the same black jumpsuit you wore on the boat from Jagajaga to Ọrun, you pull Brother Fatai's jacket on. Hood up, head down, you risk it and jog to Nirvana's place.

———✺———

Within fifteen minutes, you are at Nirvana's building.

She is waiting by the entrance so that you don't have to scan your face to be let in. Leaning against the wall beside the door, she smiles when you walk up.

"Amen?" she asks, her voice gently sonorous, deeper than her lean frame would suggest.

You smile and nod but take your hood off only after you've entered the warmly lit space of her apartment. The savoury scent of stew welcomes you. Nirvana promised you dinner, and it appears that she's following through. Hunger gnaws at your stomach. You had been too nervous to eat the shelter supper of beans and yam, and now you are famished.

Nirvana takes your coat, and her fingers run down your arm. When she serves and hands you a plate of golden brown fried plantain topped with tomato stew, her fingers graze yours. When she sits across from you at the small glass hexagonal dining table, her knees brush against yours. The whole time her eyes are fixed on your face. With a fork midway to her mouth, she asks what you do for work.

"Before I came here, I was a teacher and a dancer."

"When did you come here?"

"About nine months ago . . ."

"You like it?"

You are silent for two mouthfuls of food and a long drink of sweet water, then you carefully respond, "It's like a tomb with a beautiful mural on the outside wall."

Nirvana's eyebrows shoot up her forehead. She chokes on her plantain in laughter.

"That's dark and deep," she exclaims.

You do not laugh; instead, you ask, "Where are you from, Nirvana?"

"Born and raised in this tomb." She wrinkles her nose and bites a corner of her lower lip. And your face falls into your palms, you laugh. "Sorry to insult your home!"

"It's all good. It's definitely a fucked-up place, but it's the only home I know."

Your knees brush against each other again, and this time neither of you move away. You lean into it. There are many reasons you shouldn't be here, many reasons you should be under the scratchy covers at the shelter, shrivelled in fear, crying for Chichi Girl and Ẹbun Mimọ, praying to see Lailai again, praying that a caseworker will take particular interest in your situation sooner than seven months. But you want to be seen. You unzip the high collar of your jumpsuit, past your throat and midway down your sternum.

You are foolish, but you want to be seen, and touched, and to remember that you are alive, now, in this body of yours—before they come for you, because isn't it inevitable? You trace the Sịṣa on the back of your hands, up your arms; you look up and ask Nirvana, "You have a fetish?"

Her pale eyes widen, taken aback. A shy smile spreads across her angular face. "No. Maybe—no, I don't know. I just find you incredibly beautiful. I mean, seeing your face now . . . yeah . . ."

You shrug and shake your head, "It's okay if you have a fetish; anyway, beauty isn't good for anything—you can't eat it."

Nirvana smiles wide and it makes her eyes half moons. She touches your hands and traces your Sịṣa.

She says, "I can try."

She spends the night trying. You are eager lovers, and you cry from relief when she finally flexes her fingers inside you. She bites your jewelled breast, and you come quickly, a fierce rushing that makes you think of the ocean at home.

You don't intend to, but you fall asleep entangled in the sheets of her plush bed. When you wake up, it is early morning. She brings you a cup of hot milky tea and shows you a picture on her screen. It is of you, curled into a tight ball, your dark skin, your Sịsa, stark against the pale grey of her bedding. She took it hours ago. You feel air dispel from your chest; the picture was automatically timed and geotagged. You look at her aghast, snatch the screen from her hands and try to delete it, but it doesn't recognize your fingerprints, it won't respond to you.

Your voice strains in a hoarse whisper as you ask, "What have you done?!"

Nirvana stutters, "I-I'm sorry, I should have asked, it's analog, don't worry, I just wanted to remember."

"Nothing is analog, Nirvana! Memories are here." You gesture to your temple, then the centre of your chest.

You hand her the phone, demanding that she delete the picture, but you know it's too late, it has been tagged for hours. They have already found you.

Before the Authorities cuff and lead you out of Nirvana's apartment, you tell her, "You know from my Sịsa, I'm from Jagajaga. My name is Ife; it means Love."

<hr />

You wouldn't be able to tell how long you sat, naked, in that glass box; a box not unlike the body scanner at the Port, but much smaller. Too small to stretch your arms out to their full extent. And it might have been your mind fucking with you, but it seemed to shrink as time progressed. It grew smaller as you waited indefinitely at the detention centre that sat overlooking the ocean on the edge of the city. You had been processed quickly, scanned by a massive eye with its orange light and dinged as blank, unregistered, slum scum.

The Authority officer had asked how you got to Ọrun, and you'd told him everything except for your time at Femme Circle. If he'd believed you, he hadn't shown it. His features had stayed blank as he'd recorded your story. He'd asked if you were selling sex unregistered when they picked you up. "No," you'd said, "I was on a date." You thought his eyes had dimmed with sadness, but it might have been your mind fucking with you. Then he'd read you your rights, which were that you had none and that you would be held indefinitely until an arrangement to pay your fine was made, or until you were registered by an Ọrun citizen in good standing.

So you wouldn't be able to tell how long you sat, naked, in that glass box, snug against another glass box that held another woman, on top of another glass box with another woman, a hive of glass boxes with blank people stuck between home and Ọrun. You don't cry, you don't pray, you just count your breath and surrender.

Then they release you. And you find out it's been two weeks.

A different Authority officer tells you you've been registered by one Vana Maina, an Ọrun citizen in good standing. When he hands you your jumpsuit, Brother Fatai's jacket, and the phone, he adds under his breath, "Lucky slum slut, must've been a good fuck."

You pretend not to hear. You are stunned.

Outside, Nirvana is waiting by a yellow bicycle, holding a gold helmet. She offers you a tentative smile, and you respond by saying, "You don't own me now."

"No, no, of course, I would never, I don't want that . . . I'm sorry, I didn't know."

Your body starts to tremble as though a fault line in the

foundation of your core has shifted. You begin to collapse, and Nirvana catches you, but you push her off and stand on your own, still shaking. "You don't own me," you say again.

"I know."

"I will you pay you back for the registration."

"You can't, I don't want you to."

"How much did it cost?"

"It doesn't matter. I was stupid and fucked you up. It's only right that I fix it."

"You don't own me."

"I know. I'm sorry . . . I didn't know."

You cry into your palms, awash in relentless waves of grief, relief, gratitude, and guilt.

Nirvana stands close to you without touching you. She says, "You're registered now, you're free to come and go, the port is open to you."

"Thank you," you hiccup. You lift your face from your palms and look into her face. "Thank you."

She shrugs and shakes her head. After you catch your breath and the tears start drying on your sunken cheeks, you both look toward the sea, water thrashing against the rocks. On this side, the ocean is harsh.

"What will you do now?" Nirvana asks.

You think. You see Lailai's face before yours, you hear Chichi Girl crying, you remember Ẹbun Mimọ praying to Yemaya. You think of all those cameras scanning you now, imagine having your own profile: *Ife Kobo. Registered Worker.* You turn to face the detention building with your chin up, looking directly at as many cameras as you can spot.

Turning back to Nirvana, you tell her your decision.

LEANNE TOSHIKO SIMPSON

MONSTERS

The man I'm about to marry tells the party that the shooter had a family history of mental illness, and everyone but me nods knowingly because I am too busy thinking that the floor is lava.

There is no safe way to leave this room. Fifty-eight people are dead on the Las Vegas Strip and I feel obliged to apologize for a stranger's brutality or risk being painted with the same brush. He reaches for my hand, but my nails have already dug a trench in my palm. I pretend to be sorry for bleeding on the hostess's white leather couch, but I secretly think the party could use more colour.

There are days where I forgive myself for my illness, but there are also days where the air will shatter if I exhale too quickly. Yesterday, when I told him there were monsters in my face, he pulled my fingers out of my eyes and held me until I remembered to be scared of myself. *Do you still recognize me?* he asked. I nodded, squeezing the skin between his fingers to make sure I still fit. I was afraid to ask him if he was scared too.

Today, I think he is scared that people will see the mess as he carefully dabs the blood from my hands. I want to touch everything, leave a little bit of my disaster on every person in the room. I want to tell them that I do not appreciate how my illness is only allowed at the dinner table after lives have been destroyed. I don't want to talk about it now. The headlines have already spoken for me.

They say when you marry someone, you also marry their family, but I'm not worried about that. I'm scared of marrying his privilege. I'm scared of having to explain to someone who loves me that people like me are more likely to be victims of violence than perpetrators, and conversations like these are why I'm scared to book time off from work for my psychiatrist.

I am not good company.

He gently excuses us from the party, then says he loves me when we're safely in the car. His mouth exhales beautiful shapes like blown glass, but his eyes say *I love this sad broken girl in spite of herself* and I am so tired of being carried when I can walk.

He's never seen me angry before, not like this. I'm screaming and sobbing and throwing my body over his and I need him to know it's because he's wrong and not because I'm sick.

Afterwards, I run my thumbs across his cheeks and search his face for landmarks. *Do you still recognize me?* he says, and I nod. His lips find small shards of hope buried in the cavity of my palm. *Do you still recognize me?* I ask, and this time I am not afraid, not even on the quiet ride home.

TROY SEBASTIAN
/NUPQU ʔAK·ⱵAṂ

TAX NIʔ PIK̇AK (A LONG TIME AGO)

Tax niʔ Pik̇ak—a long time ago, Ka titi was in her kitchen when Uncle Pat came in and said:

"Did you see what the suyupi did now? They built a statue to David Thompson. They say he is a great man. Many people gathered at the hilltop and there were speeches and ka·pi. I like ka·pi, so I went there and that's what they said."

Uncle Pat was known for a few things, his old beat-up red-and-black Ford truck and his love of ka·pi.

"If you keep drinking that it will make you think like a crazy suyupi," said Ka titi.

It was true, Uncle Pat had become more and more like the suyupi with every cup of ka·pi. He used to dream with KⱵawⱵa and Kupi, but ever since he enjoyed too much ka·pi they dreamt on their own.

"Ka·pi is for ceremony and blessings," said Ka titi.

"Every day is a blessing," Uncle Pat said as he rummaged in the ka·pi can for a hint of brew.

Ka titi stood at the kitchen window looking out toward the bones of Yawuʔnik̓.

"I tell you something that you don't know," said Ka titi.

"Oh what's that," said Uncle Pat.

"Ever since the white man showed up on teevee, a lot of us Indians don't believe in miracles. Unless Alex Trebek shakes your hand or Pat Paycheck gives you a spin, there is no magic to be had."

"Uh-huh."

"David Thompson was hungry, lost, and afraid when he came to Ktunaxa ʔamak̓is and that's how he should be remembered. Instead, we get this story that celebrates him as some great explorer, and that is wrong. He didn't know where he was going."

"Oh ya," said Uncle Pat, listening in the way that men do and do not.

"Well that's not what they say in town," he continued.

"Uh-huh," said Ka titi.

"And that's not what's in the newspaper."

"Uh-huh," said Ka titi.

"They said they are going to name the new school for him too. Maybe even change the name of the Overwaitea to the David Thompson Memorial Overwaitea."

"ɬa taʔqna," said Ka titi.

"That's what they are saying," said Uncle Pat.

Ka titi had been alive longer than most of the people on the reserve. She remembered when David Thompson arrived in Ktunaxa ʔamak̓is and she wasn't impressed then and she wasn't impressed now.

Uncle Pat had managed to scrounge enough ka·pi grounds to fix together a half a cup. He put the kettle on the stove and waited for it to boil.

Ka titi waited for the kettle. As she waited, her thoughts took her away. Sometimes her thoughts brought her to places where she had been long before and places that she hadn't been to at all but still could remember. Her thoughts were some-where between the first glacier winter and the first *Hockey Night in Canada*.

The whistling kettle brought her back to the present as Uncle Pat poured the boiling water into the cup he had placed on the counter.

Uncle Pat headed to the outhouse to do his business expect-ing to enjoy that lovely, hot cup of ka·pi when he returned.

He must have been in the outhouse a long time as it was getting dark when he got out. On the way back, he thought he heard Kupi call his name. This scared Uncle Pat, so he ran into the house.

Ka titi was sitting at the kitchen table with his cup of ka·pi in her old hands and a small pile of smokes next to a well-used cigarette lighter.

"Kupi called my name," said Uncle Pat, scared and filled with the heebie-jeebies.

"Sure she did, you are not the only one to use the outhouse."

"I'm not?"

"Waha. Think of all the ancestors who are in these woods, where do you think they go?"

That had not occurred to Uncle Pat. In that contemplation, Ka titi put a smoke to her mouth, lit the tobacco, and took a long drag.

Uncle Pat had not seen Ka titi smoke before, and that along with the call of Kupi really put him in a state.

Ka titi handed a smoke to Uncle Pat and told him to take a drag and give it to the moon. Only then could he smoke it for himself. Uncle Pat heeded her direction and went outside giving his smoke to kǿiɬmitiɬnuqka.

It was good to give the smoke to kǿiɬmitiɬnuqka as it was just coming up behind papa ʔa·kwukɬiʔit. The buzz from the ka·pi had left Uncle Pat, and his eyes were clearing up.

"It sure is beautiful," said Uncle Pat.

"It sure is beautiful," answered Kupi.

Uncle Pat did not see Kupi near him when he smoked. He was so surprised he nearly dropped his smoke. He offered Kupi the smoke, but Kupi laughed like an old bird and flew off toward Bonners.

"Crazy bird," said Uncle Pat.

He took another smoke and gave it to papa ʔa·kwukɬiʔit and headed back inside.

Ka titi was still sitting at the kitchen table when Uncle Pat came in. She took the cigarette roller, looked at it, and put it back into its buckskin case.

"Kupi didn't like to smoke," said Uncle Pat.

Ka titi looked at Uncle Pat: "ɬa taʔqna."

"I know, Ka titi."

"Let me tell you about David Thompson," said Ka titi. "He wasn't just lost, he was a copycat."

Uncle Pat listened to Ka titi, eyeing the ka·pi swirling around the cup in Ka titi's hand.

"David Thompson heard the story of your Uncle Skin and was trying to do the same thing," said Ka titi.

"What are you talking about," asked Uncle Pat.

"Your Uncle Skin," said Ka titi. "What, you think you are the only uncle around here?"

"Well . . ."

"There have been many uncles before you and many more are still to come."

"Oh well."

"And David Thompson heard of your uncle's tale and tried to do the same thing."

"What story is that, Ka titi," asked Uncle Pat.

"Your Uncle Skin has been missing for a long time."

"Yes, Ka titi."

"He wasn't always missing, you know. He used to go missing, but he would always come back, usually around jump dance and the rodeos."

Uncle Pat just listened to Ka titi speak. He never knew his Uncle Skin, and any time folks talked about him, Uncle Pat would get quiet and listen.

"Your Uncle Skin was crazy, not like the suyupi with their cars and their ka·pi. He was crazy like numa in ɬumayitnamu. He knew things that were happening far away and he knew things before they happened. He was a clever man, but that made others in the tribe wary of him. He was often seen walking with Kupi on nights like this.

"One day the tribe had been without a good meal in a long time. Hunting season was over and there was little game to eat. So Skin started walking. At first it seemed like he was walking in a trance. But he soon found his way over the mountains to the east, towards the kuɸkiyawiy. Everyone thought he wouldn't come back, as most of our men who went that way got tangled up in rodeos and love triangles.

"That's not what happened to Uncle Skin. He walked from here at ?aq̓am, through the mountains to the plains, all the way to a place called Lethbridge. When he got there, the suyupis were opening a brand new Overwaitea. They were just about to eat when he walked in the store and asked for food. As these suyupi had never seen a Ktunaxa before they were naturally impressed as we Ktunaxa are known for our well-developed bodies and easygoing attitude towards sex."

"I'll say," said Uncle Pat.

"Anyhow, Skin made his way to the deli and asked for a beet salad and some chicken. The suypui didn't know what to do so they gave it to him. He put it into a buckskin bag and headed west.

"The suyupi were so impressed by his feat of courage that they began to tell stories about him. They built a statue in his honour and this is what David Thompson learned of in his London condo."

"Uh-huh."

"When Skin came back to the tribe, everyone was hungry and some of us were really irritable. Just the sight of him was enough to upset the tribe as there was just enough food for everyone until spring.

"Nasu?kin saw Skin and said, 'Waha, Skin! We don't want you here. You have been gone too long and we hardly recognize you. Ka titi thought you were ku¢kiyawiy and wanted to shoot you.'"

"You did?" asked Uncle Pat.

"It is true," said Ka titi. "I was younger then and prone to bad judgment.

"Skin raised his hand and began to speak. 'It is true, Nasu?kin. I have been gone for too long. You don't recognize me and I hardly recognize you too. I had to listen to Kupi to tell me who is who.'

"The tribe was surprised at this and some rumbling began.

"'But behold,' said Skin. He rummaged into his buckskin bag and pulled out the deli chicken and the beet salad.

"'I have gone a long distance and have come back with food for the tribe. The suyupis over the mountain have built a new Overwaitea and they gifted this to us.'

"Nasu?kin took a look at the food and the eyes of the ?aq‡smaknik̓ and said, 'Sometimes Kupi knows what is best for the tribe. You have done well, Skin. We have enough food to keep us through winter.'

"The tribe had a big feast that night and everyone was tired with red-mouthed snores. Skin knew that the tribe would not trust him any longer, so he left his clothes folded on the bridge to town and flew off into the night.

"Years later, David Thompson arrived and started the mess we are in today."

"Hola! That is some story, Ka titi," said Uncle Pat. "Is it true?"

"Listen for the coming of Kupi and they will tell you what is true. They are better than newspapers and teevee. But don't talk to them or you will fly off like your Uncle Skin.

"And that is why we Ktunaxa don't speak to Kupi at night."

HAJERA KHAJA

WAITING FOR ADNAN

t is 8:00 p.m. and Adnan has not yet arrived. Maryam is sitting cross-legged on the sofa. Her mother is at the dining table, fingering the edge of the heavy plastic tablecloth.

"Are you sure he said 7:00 p.m.?" Maryam's mother asks, tense lines cutting across her forehead.

Maryam tucks a finger inside her hijab and wiggles it around. The safety pin has already left a small curvy imprint in the soft flesh above her throat.

"Maybe he said Sunday?"

"He'll be here soon," Maryam says. Her eyes wander to the rug on the floor. She had vacuumed it earlier that afternoon, trying to pick up all the white bits of heel dust sprinkled about like dandruff. She catches a small speck, about the size of a cumin seed, half-hidden under the sofa. "Your feet are too dry," she tells her mother, bending down to pick up the fleck of dead skin. "You shed while you walk."

Her mother sighs. "I'll go clean up till he comes," she says.

Brown splotches of dried curry are splattered near the foot of the stove and chopped-up bits of mint and cilantro are pressed into the hazy grey tiles. There is a lingering scent of burnt oil in the air, even though Maryam had walked around with a can of air freshener after her mother had finished cooking, sending bursts of citrus-scented aerosol particles throughout the house.

In the kitchen, her mother gets down on all fours, dragging the green bits together with a wet sponge.

<hr />

Maryam jaywalked across the road, half-running, half-teetering on the pointed heel of her boots. She had asked Adnan to meet her at 6:00 p.m. at the Second Cup across from Seneca College where she worked as an instructor in the ESL program. It was more than twenty minutes past the hour when she yanked open the entrance door. "I am so so sorry," she said, the words rushing out as she unfurled a scarf from around her neck and plopped herself into a chair.

Adnan pushed a coffee cup toward her. "I bought you a latte, but it's probably cold by now."

Maryam took a sip. It tasted watery and bitter but was still warm. She apologized again, explaining that she was held up by some students who had questions about an assignment due the next day. It was clear to her that they hadn't started, but she felt bad to brush them away.

"I hate people like that, acting all entitled," Adnan said.

Maryam shrugged her shoulders. "Listen," she said, "I told my dad about you and he's agreed to meet you." She pushed her lips back in a fake grin and stuck up both thumbs.

Adnan started playing with his empty cup, rotating it with one hand and strumming on it with the other. "So soon?" he said, looking at her momentarily. "It's only been a month."

"I want to be sure they approve before things get too serious."

Adnan stopped playing with his cup.

"If, I mean," Maryam added, "if they get serious."

"Why not cross that bridge when we get there?"

A gurgle of hunger escaped from Maryam's stomach. Her feet felt cramped and sweaty inside her boots. They were a half-size too small but at seventy per cent off, she couldn't resist the purchase. "I can't move forward without a green light," she said.

Adnan raised an eyebrow.

"They haven't met you yet. They're still at a yellow light."

Later that night, when Maryam was already in bed, her phone twitched and lit up. It was a message from Adnan: *I'll be happy to meet your fam. Sorry if I was a jerk earlier. Had a rough day.*

Maryam forwarded the message to her sister, Aisha. *Analysis?* she added.

Dude must be really into you, Aisha wrote back, then sent a smiling-face emoji with two hearts in place of the eyes.

⸎

At 8:22 p.m., Maryam hears a car turn into their driveway. *Finally here,* she taps into her phone.

Aisha replies: *So no car accident + coma? Would've at least made for a romantic story to tell your kids.*

Maryam sends her an eye-rolling emoji.

Adnan smells like rubbing alcohol. He hands Maryam's mother an unwrapped bouquet of yellow daffodils and presents Maryam with a Godiva gift bag. Maryam's father comes down the stairs wearing a beige sports coat over a black turtleneck. Maryam and her mother exchange looks. Her father hates sports coats and only wears them on special occasions. He glances at the watch on his wrist before taking Adnan's outstretched hand.

Adnan drops down on one knee to undo his shoelaces and remarks how busy the DVP is, even on weekends. "But thank God for Indian Standard Time," he says, peering up, a wide grin smeared over his face.

⸎

Maryam's father squinted his eyes against the glare of the computer screen. "Is *accomplishment* spelled with one *c* or two?"

"Two," Maryam said.

"I knew that," he muttered, his finger coming down hard on the keyboard. He rolled his chair back and looked up. "My spell check isn't working for some reason."

"Can you please be nice to Adnan when he comes?" Maryam said.

Her father rolled his tongue around inside his mouth.

"I'm serious, you need to stop getting all fundo on everyone."

"Fundo to you is commitment to me."

"And there are other ways to show you're committed."

Her father rolled his chair back into the desk. "*Commitment.* Two *m*s or two *t*s?" he asked, searching the screen.

"Two *m*s." Maryam tugged on a droopy yellow leaf curling down from the shoot of a bamboo plant.

"That leaf's got life in it still. It would have come off otherwise."

Maryam yanked it hard and the plant fell sideways, wet stones spilling onto the desk. "Or you can just snap the life out of it," she said, picking the plant back up.

Her father covered the puddle of water with a newspaper. "Did you know you can use newspapers to dry wet shoes?"

Maryam stood up. "So you don't trust my judgment at all?"

"What's his name again?"

Maryam raised her eyes to the ceiling. "Adnan Syed."

Her father smirked. "Like the guy from *Serial*?"

"Except that he hasn't been accused of murdering anyone, which is good enough for me."

"Then your standards are too low."

"And yours are too high. We have to meet in the middle or we'll be doing this till I'm sixty!"

"I'll be dead by then. Most likely." Her father did the tongue-rolling thing again.

"Dad." Maryam placed both hands on the desk. "Please. Give him a fair chance."

"Ask him to come after Eid. I don't want him ruining your Eid if I don't like him."

When Maryam sent Aisha a thumbs-down emoji as a summary of the conversation in her father's office, Aisha wrote back: *Dad will be Dad. But you could always elope*, with a winking smiley face.

Maryam jabbed into her phone: *Thanks for the help drama queen!*

Maryam's father suggests praying Isha before dinner.

"But it's getting late, no?" her mother says. Her father looks at Adnan, who is about to sit down.

"I don't mind," Adnan says.

Maryam lays out the prayer mats on the ground. Her father places a hand on Adnan's back and nudges him forward to lead.

When they finish, Maryam's father turns around and Adnan copies the motion.

"How much Quran do you have memorized?" her father asks.

Adnan glances at Maryam. "Not much," he says. "An okay amount."

"How much is not much?"

"Just the usual, whatever I learnt growing up. Most of the thirtieth para."

"You read well. You should learn more. And you pray five times, of course?"

"Yes. Of course."

"You wake up for fajr every day?"

"Mostly, yes."

"Meaning?"

Maryam clenches her jaw.

"Sorry?"

"What does *mostly* mean?"

"I sleep through my alarm sometimes."

"How often?"

"Dad—" Maryam says quietly. Her mother places a hand on Maryam's knee.

"Maybe once a week. Sometimes more. But usually less."

Maryam's father continues to question Adnan. Her eyes dart back and forth between them, as if they're stuck in a game of hot potato.

When Maryam is sure at least half an hour has passed since they have finished prayer, she touches her mother's elbow lightly.

"I'm going to get dinner ready," her mother says, getting up. "You men please wrap up your discussion."

In the kitchen, Maryam flaps her arms, trying to air out her sticky armpits. She raises an arm above her head and sniffs.

"Here, taste this," her mother says, pulling out a wooden spoon from a pot filled with golden brown curry. She drags a finger against the bottom of the spoon and wipes it on the tip of Maryam's tongue.

"Spicy," Maryam says. "Too spicy."

"Good. It's for Adnan, not you."

Maryam bites her lower lip.

Her mother pats her face. "If Allah wants, he will be your husband and no one can stop that. If not, then He has someone better written for you."

Maryam looks around the kitchen. "What can I take?"

"I'll manage. Go wash your face. You look tense," her mother says, lifting the pot and tilting it toward a large serving bowl, a film of steam fogging up her glasses as the hot curry gushes out.

Maryam's mother asks Adnan to tell them about his family. She places a bowl of curry in front of him and motions to Maryam to pass the naans.

Adnan says his parents live in Dubai, his father is an architect and his mother is an interior designer. They visit him for two weeks every summer and spend the winter holidays in Miami, where his brother lives with his family.

"Do you like Dubai?" Maryam's mother asks.

Adnan says there isn't much to do apart from shopping and eating at overpriced restaurants with only brown servers. "The life there is so"—he pauses and stares at the ceiling— "bourgeois. And the state of the foreign workers is horrifying. I don't care to go back."

Maryam sniffs and wipes the edges of her nostrils with a folded tissue.

"Is the food too spicy for you?" Adnan asks, one side of his mouth stretched into a half-smile.

"The people who live there allow for the injustice," Maryam's father says to his plate.

Adnan scrunches his forehead. He is quiet for a moment and then says, "What do you mean?"

"Everyone plays a part. No one is free from blame."

Maryam looks at Adnan pleadingly. His eyes are squinted, his mouth set into a tight line.

"You're right," Adnan says. "We live on stolen land so that also makes us responsible for the suicide crisis that's happening in Attawapiskat right now."

Maryam's father bites into a samosa, bits of flaky crust falling into his plate. He stares at the painting on the wall in front of him, above where Maryam and her mother are sitting. It is an abstract painting, a splatter of greens and blues, resembling dense foliage. Aisha had chosen it on a family trip to IKEA more than ten years ago.

"You're passionate about social justice issues," Maryam's father says to the painting.

Adnan sits taller and turns to face him. "Yes, yes I am."

"I don't believe in them."

"You don't believe in justice?"

"Not in the way you young people go about it. If you were downtown today, it would have taken you a while to get out of the city with the DVP all clogged up. Black Lives Matter was doing a sit-in on Dundas again. What I don't understand is how they think they can achieve anything by disrupting traffic and just shouting for justice."

Adnan reaches for a glass of water and drowns it all in one go.

"Have some biryani, Adnan," Maryam's mother says. "You've hardly eaten."

Maryam's father stands up, his chair screeching as it drags on the hardwood floor. "I have some work to get to. Please excuse me." He turns to face Adnan, bowing his head slightly. "Nice meeting you. Please give our salaams to your parents."

"Dad," Maryam says, "stay till dessert."

Her father looks at her, his eyes droopy and his cheeks sagging, as if the muscles holding them in place have suddenly gone lax. "No dessert for me tonight, thank you," he says quietly.

※

For their first meetup, Maryam suggested coffee after work, but Adnan insisted on lunch. They settled on Paramount, a Middle Eastern restaurant a short walk away from Mount Sinai Hospital, where Adnan worked in the IT department. Maryam wore her favourite boots—a pair of calf-length, caramel-brown Jimmy Choos—over navy blue skinny jeans and a knee-length dusky rose swing dress that fluttered about as she walked. Her beige and white paisley print hijab matched the colour of her boots.

By the time Maryam got to the restaurant, Adnan was already there waiting for her. He stood up to greet her, his face breaking out into a wide smile, teeth white as plaster, framed by a thin goatee. His hair was long and wavy, curling around his ears like inverted commas.

Arabic music bubbled out of the overhead speakers, the singer's voice thick and mournful. Adnan commented on the vibrancy of the music.

"I'm more of a Coldplay, Mumford & Sons kind of person," Maryam said.

"Coffee shop music?"

"Yes, that's it, exactly." Maryam tilted her head. "I never thought of it as a genre but it works."

They talked non-stop for over two hours. Maryam learnt that Adnan grew up in Dubai, but his parents wanted him and his brother to settle elsewhere, preferably America. "But they had a very colonized attitude about things, I realize now," Adnan said, waving a small triangle of pita bread in the air. "Not through any fault of their own, of course, it was just ingrained in them. Even our vacations were restricted to Europe and North America." He's been thinking he might like to live in Malaysia for a bit. "It's one of the most advanced Muslim nations."

Maryam said she loved the idea of travelling. "My father decided to start his Ph.D. when I was in middle school. We hardly went on vacations after that."

Adnan's hands were buried in his lamb shank, greasy with fat as he pulled chunks of meat off the bone and piled them on top of a hill of saffron-stained rice. He admitted he took up interests like fads. A few years ago, he ran a full marathon with no prior running experience and only three months of training. Then there was the time he volunteered for more than twenty hours each week, helping his city councillor get re-elected. His latest obsession was reading obscure works of African literature.

Maryam said she used to read a lot in high school, but the habit fell away when she started university.

"Maybe I can suggest a few titles and we can discuss them sometime," Adnan said. He had long dark lashes that cast a slight shadow under his eyes when he blinked.

Maryam wrote down the titles on the back of a scrunched-up Aldo receipt—*The Palm-Wine Drinkard* by Amos Tutuola; *Maru* by Bessie Head; *Maps* by Nuruddin Farah. On the fourth title, her pen ran out of ink, and she couldn't make out the words when she looked at the receipt at home, only a scratchy imprint of where the letters had been pressed into the paper.

The next day, a fifty-dollar Amazon gift card arrived in her email. *To reintroduce you to the delights of reading,* read the message accompanying the card. Maryam bit the inside edges of her lips, trying not to smile into the phone. She was invigilating an exam for a colleague who had called in sick. *To reintroduce you to the delights of reading,* she read again and sent a screenshot of the email to Aisha. She scanned the small room, her eyes landing on a man with red-framed glasses, furtively glancing at his neighbour's desk.

Didn't he pay for lunch too? Aisha wrote back.

So?

Feels a bit much.

Remember that hadith about how all our souls were alive before we were born, and how when you meet someone you knew in that other life, you feel an instant connection to them?

I know where you're going with this, but

It didn't feel like I was meeting him for the first time. It was like I was just being reintroduced to him.

Beware of the first impression! It can wear off. You shld know that.

Maryam looked up from her phone. The man who was cheating had his back pressed against his chair and was scribbling hurriedly without looking down, his eyes locked on his neighbour's papers. *I think he might be a keeper,* she wrote back.

Adnan gets up to leave, saying he has some work to finish up and a busy day tomorrow as well. Maryam and her mother wait on the porch as Adnan backs out of the driveway. He rolls down the window to wave goodbye before driving away. Someone in the neighbourhood is burning firewood and Maryam's stomach rises and falls as she breathes in the singed air. Her mother wraps her arms around Maryam's waist. "Let's go inside, it's chilly," she says.

Upstairs, the hallway is dark except for an orange slab of light spilling out from underneath her father's office. Maryam lifts her hand to knock but her knuckles touch the door without making a sound. She waits, but doesn't hear anything from inside, no keyboard clatter, no creaking chair, only the sounds of her mother's movements in the kitchen downstairs, pots clanging, the tap running full stream.

On her desk, a white light is blinking from Maryam's phone. There's a missed video call from Aisha, and before that, a long list of message notifications from her:

Where's my realtime news feed?

You're killing me! Has the grilling commenced???

Does he look handsome?

Gah why are you doing this to me!!!

Bedtime for the kids so I'm pausing on the harassment. But I expect full deets tmrw!

Maryam dismisses the notifications and leaves the phone on her desk, next to the books that had arrived from Amazon a few weeks ago, their covers glossy and spines still uncracked. She buries herself in the pile of Indian suits on her bed, which she had emptied that morning from a bin at the bottom of her closet. The smell of moth balls makes her throat squeeze and her eyes water.

After Aisha got married, their father made Maryam promise she wouldn't think about marriage until she found a job and had a steady career path laid out in front of her. Maryam agreed without hesitating. She was in her first year of undergrad and stayed late at the library every night so she could study without being interrupted by the tense discussions happening at home between Aisha and their father. They were both stubborn, but Aisha was also feverishly in love. She even got Imran's parents to call their father repeatedly, begging him to agree. When Aisha got pregnant in her final semester, she confirmed their father's worst fears—she managed to graduate, but had no drive or energy to look for a job. "If anything happens now," he said, "Aisha won't have anything to fall back on."

By the time Maryam was ready to start thinking about marriage, she found her father had hardened over the years, stiffening up to every guy she introduced to him. He found her sitting on the porch one afternoon after he had rejected an old friend of hers from university. Aamir was technically a hafidh, earning the distinction when he was fourteen, but he didn't like to call himself that anymore. They had lost touch after university and he had emailed Maryam out of the blue asking her if she was taken, and if not, if they could chat and see if there was any potential between them. "Boys are too unstable these days," her father said, placing a hand on Maryam's head as he walked past her. "When the right guy comes along, you'll thank me." Since then Maryam kept oscillating between two fears—that the right guy would never come along, or that when he did, her father would not recognize him.

⸺⸺ ✥ ⸺⸺

Monday morning, Maryam's car refuses to start, wheezing and coughing and then shutting off abruptly. Her father comes out of the house in his pyjamas and a flannel robe, belt wrapped tightly around his waist.

"Leave the keys with me," he says as Maryam emerges from the car. "I'll get my mechanic to take a look at it."

Maryam works her fingers into the chocolate leather gloves he got her for Eid.

"Do you need a ride to the subway? I just need a few minutes to change." A gust of wind slams into him and he digs his chin deeper into his robe.

"No thanks," she mutters.

"Don't forget your scarf. It's supposed to snow today."

Maryam pulls out a scarf from her bag and tosses it around her neck. She says salaam, walking past her father without looking at him.

"Walaikum assalaam," he calls out cheerfully.

Bits of snow begin to swirl and float through the air, coming down like confetti from the sky. Maryam walks fast, the platform heel of her boots clapping against the pavement. She feels a hollow burn in her stomach from drinking coffee first thing in the morning and remembers the way Adnan smiled at her when he realized her mother had made the food too spicy for her. She fiddles with the phone in her pocket, rotating it over and over.

On the bus that will take her to the subway, Maryam squeezes into the window seat of the last row. She yanks off her gloves, pulls out her phone, and starts writing a message: *Salaam Adnan. Sorry things didn't go well on Sat. If you're still interested, I'd like to chat. Let me know pls.* Her thumb hovers over the green letters for a moment, and then she whispers, "Bismillah" and hits Send. Outside, the snow has picked up, accumulating like a thin carpet on the sidewalks. It reminds Maryam of the stubble on her father's cheeks this morning. His hair is still mostly grey, but his beard has a distinct whiteness to it already, making him look older than he really is.

When her phone vibrates, Maryam feels her stomach churn. Adnan writes back: *Salaam Maryam, thx for your msg. I'd like that too. 6pm at Second Cup?*

As if on autopilot, Maryam replies: *Perfect. See you then.* She releases a long breath and lets the phone fall into her lap. She closes her eyes to block the image, but hovering before her is her father in his slippers and pyjamas, bracing himself against the cold wind.

JASON JOBIN

THEY WOULD POUR US INTO BOXES

I drive through Florida's runny orange dawn, only car on the road, streets empty and slick with heat. One of those new pandemic neighbourhoods. Where is everybody? Around the last corner I see Bob out front of his Airbnb, first sign of life, the irony. He stands with one foot on the sidewalk, one in the road, hands in fists. Bob's dying of cancer. I pull up close enough that he takes a step back. I'm supposed to ask about the accommodations. How he's doing. If he's happy with the process. I want to jump from the car and choke him, have him scratch at my hands, hasten the whole stupid production. We all sometimes need soothing. Bob slides his thin body into the car and settles his shoulders with a canine shiver. A red kerchief loops his neck, the long ends like two burnt leaves that he tugs on in turn. We scan the yolky sky through the windshield. Forecast is clear and windless. The heat's rising. Ideal conditions for our little trip. And there's the feeling—as I nudge the car into gear—that *once* I nudge the car into gear, I won't be able to stop or pull up or claim it wasn't my fault.

—

The plan had been to knock on Bob's door that first day months earlier and change his life. Me the pro, the tough one, veteran in the end-of-life gift industry. Wishes. Did anyone ever get what they wanted? I sat in the company Lexus on the street next to Bob's shrivelled mauve house, pretending to be late. I always pretended to be late. Hot Minneapolis rain biffed down the windows. Again in the Midwest. People died more in the Midwest. Something needed to be done. McDonald's wrappers and coffee cups and official-looking consent forms and contract documents carpeted the floor on the passenger side. But my suit; my suit I'd had dry cleaned that day, water-smooth lapels, deep navy, tailored to my bones. Now empowered to knock on Bob's door and make it all come true, give him exactly what he wanted. I'd put through his paperwork that morning, against every instinct made it official.

Dead grass surrounded Bob's house. He had a blue Toyota with a bumper sticker of a wolf's face. A bathroom sink sat plunged in the middle of his lawn like it had landed from a great height. Maybe redecorating; maybe a birdbath.

I uncoiled myself from the car, locked it, and walked up to the door. Knocked. Then again.

For a few seconds I got no sense anyone was home. No feel of inhabitation. But soon a shuffle of feet, breathing. A pause like someone staring at the door and deciding whether to answer it or not. The door swung in, showed a less damaged-looking version of the guy from his application's photo. How had he done the application photo? In that, he looked to have two or even three feet in the grave. Eyeliner. Makeup. The right shadows, some kind of gauzy filter, imagining the death of a loved one. Hard to say. But in person, he looked decent. Downcast eyes, sure. Something more than downcast: thrown, crash-landed. Sallow skin. Stub for a nose. Thin brown hair somehow holding on. Men with cancer never wore wigs, and here he kept to the script.

"Please, no solicitation," he said, indicating a sign stapled next to his mailbox that said as much and had a giant cartoon foot kicking a small cartoon butt.

"I'm Calvin," I said. "I work for Wishing Well."

"Wishing Well." He chewed his lip. "Wishing Well."

"You applied with us nine weeks ago."

"Oh, man. Wishing Well?"

"Yes."

"You've come to see me?"

"Yes, I wanted to talk—"

"Like, *you've come to see me*?" His eyes popped. We both could not believe it.

"I came to discuss some aspects of your application. It was very touching."

"Of course. Please come in. Come right in."

He led me to his kitchen table. I sat while he fixed two glasses of peppermint tea and talked almost to himself about the relative temperature of water you wanted for each different kind of tea—hotter for black, cooler for green, acids and tannins and flavonoids—and I really didn't give a shit. Bob's house shone as if new, fresh from the box. Smells of Lysol and hand sanitizer, undercurrent of vinegar. He'd cleaned the dust off the dust. The blue tile like deep ocean. Even the grout between the tiles looked scrubbed.

He brought the mugs of tea over and slid one to me. Steam spiralled up past our faces. I sipped and burned my tongue, pretended it was fine.

"Bob, we were all sad to hear about your illness," I said, because these were things you said.

"Cancer," he said, like a man who has used the word so much it isn't a word.

Indeed. "Indeed." I tried to wrap my head around it. How this narrative began.

"It's lymphoma," he said.

"Your letter was very touching."

"It took you nine weeks?"

No one had ever called me out. "Things aren't always light-speed for us."

"Nine weeks, for a guy like me?"

"I understand. We're late."

"It's a long time, is all."

How dare we delay. We were monsters. A pause. I stared into my tea, the liquid seeming to spin with nothing to spin it. "What I came here to talk about is, well, the wish."

"The wish," he said and leaned back with a curled smile.

"It's quite the ask."

"Oh, it's fine. I'm stupid." He swished his fingers through the tea steam, back and forth like opening a bead curtain.

"Bob, it's just civilian space travel is a complex, expensive, fledgling industry. I'll have to ask around. There are start-ups, and think tanks, all that stuff."

"Think tanks." He nodded.

"You know what I mean, right?"

"I do, I do. Just always wanted that. Maybe I was joking."

"You don't have to have been joking," I said.

"I don't want to seem ungrateful."

"Who knows, right?"

"Why me?" he said.

"Why anybody?"

He hummed at that. Bob drank most of his tea in a swallow and turned his head to peer out the window. He looked to be inspecting the glass for imperfections. The house had cooled around us. "I'll be right back," he said. Bob left the kitchen, disappeared down the hall. The purr of a bathroom fan.

I slid from my chair, careful, listening to the bathroom sounds. Walked to the fridge. Crossword magnets (*I once met a yellow cat in the fire*), a wedding invitation to Honolulu, phone bills, cards from a brother, an uncle, none mentioning cancer. I needed something else, medical forms, receipt for a printing service, banded money, a hint of forgery. Looked then on top of the fridge: thick dust, dead spider like a small closed hand, gnarled banana tip—he hadn't cleaned everything. The bathroom fan kept on and seemed to tick, count down. Still no flush.

I moved to the drawers. Cutlery. Tea towels. Straws and paper plates. An empty one. A drawer with a replica of the CT scan he'd sent. What did that mean? Perhaps the original? Was it fake? I held it up to the light, as if the paper might hold secret holograms, watermarks, miniscule self-portraits.

Flush. Tap running.

I put everything back. Sat down and picked at my cuticles, made sure little flakes of skin fell on the table.

Bob wandered back into the kitchen, not looking at all self-conscious the way some people do when they're in the bathroom longer than a piss. Slow descent back to his chair. A subtle groan. "So, what do I do?" he said.

"You just sit tight. I've got connections with the Air Force, that new one, Escape Industries, even some at SpaceX."

"You'll be in touch?"

"Count on it. Here's my card. Call me anytime." I slid my white card across the table, but left it beyond his reach. Sick men didn't like things put right into their hands, and here I would honour that.

I drove back to my rental. The house rose up from a recently asphalted driveway, space for three cars, pubic line of grass by the mailbox. Enormous wood door with a heron's face knocker. Big, empty luxury. I parked and sat in the car for several minutes wishing the house were small and held some kind of narrative: a murder scene, room of old birds' nests, pottery kiln. I hadn't even used all the bathrooms yet. Kept finding new ones with smaller and smaller showers. One of my hands had cramped while driving, the muscles tied to something invisible and ready to give.

I left the car. Moonlit clouds like glowing lint, star haze in the gaps. My left leg had a kink around the knee. Had I fallen last night? I limped up the steps to the door and rapped the heron, my fingers around its wing. Metal echoed on wood. Struck it again, again. Did anyone live in this neighbourhood? The Russian billionaires had bought Minneapolis. They'd all come to my block party, sailed their yachts up the street. I unlocked the door and went inside. Home for now. Piles of folders slumped in the entry, other applications, the weight of them. Cancers and neurodegenerations and freakish genetic nightmares, and a real person housed in each 8.5 x 11 epi-taph. And here I doubted Bob's. Had doubted his application from the beginning. Called his oncologist even, a guy named Benleven, real friendly, said him and Bob went way back, which doctors never say.

I dodged several pairs of identical leather shoes and made my way to the kitchen. I always did my work in the kitchen.

The house mostly barren other than the items I brought with me on jobs: a book of mountain photography by Max Rive, a small brass Buddha, several soft lamps, a monocle-sized magnifying glass, a circular rug the colour and texture of an elk that a former wish recipient named Kim had willed to me (against all regulation, but I'd loved her). These items strewn across the butcher-block island and breakfast nook, the microwave, the third sink. By now grown expert at making a place look barely lived in, like a shrub clinging to a rock face. Eerie sameness everywhere I travelled. Different rooms, counters, floors, but always my silver pen, always the rug, the Buddha, my black steel file shelf, always my face inches from the kitchen table until the grey morning, cheek soon settled there, cool glass, cedar, hot oak. Spit at the corner of my mouth. Maybe sleep then. A dream about the wind in my jacket, body transformed into a balloon, floating over this ancient city with bright fires in the streets, the heat keeping me aloft but also scaring me. I floated there stuck between the fires and night's black roof. Always that dream.

I set up a video chat with Diane at the home office in New York. A woman who'd been prescribed stress balls, but who only ever chewed them, threw them at interns, or picked them to shreds with her fingernails. Her first husband had died paragliding. We all knew, but never mentioned it or referenced paragliding, and sometimes I'd see her in her office when she thought she was alone and she'd be flying her hand back and forth like when you stick it out the window of a moving car.

I loaded the chat program, heard the soft bird whistle to indicate she was there. Diane's pointy nose popped into view. Glare on her glasses, eyes invisible. Bright New York skyline the backdrop.

"If it isn't the astronaut. You look bad, Calvin."

Friendship was complicated. "I'm fine. Working this Leidel case."

"The company is really plugging it by the way."

"How bad?"

"*New York Times*, CNN, maybe a small documentary by that director who did the film about people who cut off their own ears."

"I haven't seen that one."

"No way they'd spend this much money otherwise."

"How are you?" I asked.

"Working a glioblastoma."

"Better move fast."

"I am. We're going swimming with the whale sharks." Her neck corded on the K sound.

"Lucky. That's only seasonal, right?"

"Those fucking sharks are elusive."

"Aren't they mammals?"

"It doesn't matter."

"Well, it is nice when it all works out."

A blot of silence. She pinched her cheek. "So, what's going on? No liquor stores in Minneapolis?"

"That's nice. Thank you. No, it's the guy. I don't know." I, too, slid off camera.

"You don't know what?"

"I don't know, I don't know. It's not right."

"You approved him, Calvin. That's your job." She twirled a sprig of hair around her finger until it went white.

"It's fine, I'm sure. He's got a weird attitude is all."

"He's dying. Have you died before? Maybe it's weird."

"Maybe. Maybe I just wanted to see a familiar face."

"I'm sure you regret that urge."

"How are the kids?"

"They beat each other up all the time. I think I'll allow it."

"That's good parenting."

"Hope so."

"And . . . Diane?"

"Yeah?"

"Can you keep this between us?"

"Is it actually something?"

"No, it's nothing. It's redacted. I'm stressed. Forgot my omega-3s."

"You look tired. And there's big press on your little space trip. Don't fuck it up."

"I am tired."

"Don't get close to clients. We've all done it, but you, Calvin, you have a gift. Think distance. Think a canyon. Okay?" She checked her phone, smiled a small smile.

"I'll stay far away."

"And listen, we're all reconnecting here soon, annual general, remember? Let's get tacos or something else from Mexico." But she was already thinking about other things, other tacos and sharks and body boot camps. A far-off look over my digital shoulder.

"Okay, Diane, catch you later."

"Rest up, Cal."

And again the bird whistled and the screen went dark, now with my face reflected back at me in the laptop monitor, a loose strand of hair curled into my eye, crow's feet, sheen of sweat. I took all the files for Bob from their folder and again lay them on the table. Got another drink, now with ice. The house swelled and receded in slow waves as I walked around. I circled the table, spun pieces of paper across the glass, read them aloud, orated their truth or duplicity. Soon I lay on the cold floor, shoulder blades stinging against the tile. It felt good to be flat. Tried to drink from there, spilled all over my shirt. Held Bob's CT scans up to the light and searched again for ciphers and invisible ink. They looked so real. The tumours in an elegant spread, quilted through his body like lumpy wool. A certain ticket out. Confirmation. How many people ever got that?

A few days later, Bob invited me to a local pool hall called Finnegan's. The kind of place where regulars know the story behind every broken thing. A relic business. I tiptoed down the concrete steps to the door, opened it with the sleeve of my coat. Smell of wet hands. Walked in like how you carefully pull back jungle leaves. The place was a giant L shape, subterranean and yellowed, the short side being for focused drinking, the long side for pool tables. A big curved bar polished smooth by generations of elbows. Walls the colour of tar. It reminded me of my father's basement growing up, with the plaid wallpaper and ornate dog lamps, and how he'd go down there with an expectant smile.

We took a corner table near a wall of mirrors that made the place look like multiple seedy dimensions. Bob broke the first rack and several balls stayed glued to the middle. He asked for a rebreak. Sure. Rebreaks for the dying. The next break went better. Balls spun across the felt; the four and six went down. I sipped my beer and looked at the brown-stained ceiling. Bob shot a solid, claimed solids. Missed his next shot and I was up.

Seven p.m. on a Tuesday, only four other guys were playing. A couple of old, bearded piles sat at the bar. I shot the nine, missed on the ten. Back to Bob.

"You know," he said, "always just imagine a triangle."

"Oh, yeah?"

"Yeah." He aimed his cue, sank the one in the corner.

"Like, isosceles?"

"See, you got the white ball and the object ball, and then you got the pocket. Draw that triangle in your head."

I didn't draw the triangle in my head. He went for his beer, came back to the table. Missed on the five. Said, "Fuck."

"Close one," I said.

"My dad, he always said to think of the white ball going off into infinity. Makes no sense to me. Table just ends at the railing. But he'd say that."

The game went on. We bullshitted. He had a sister, a brother. Never saw them. I had no siblings. Never saw them.

We laughed. Couldn't tell who was drinking more; around four beers I always lost track. Eventually we propped our cues against the wall, sat next to the table, and stared at the soft green felt. I wanted to lie on it, rub my cheek raw, build static. The whole room heavy by then, lidded. Years of chalk and liquor and old tanned skin.

"So," I said. "We've been looking at this company out of Florida called Javelin."

"What do they do?"

"They fly to space."

He plugged his head deeper into his neck. "Obviously."

"It's expensive, but in our range. Are you certain you want to do it?"

The eighties rock music had gotten louder, drowned out the impact of the white balls at the other tables. Conversations and glass clinking now blended to a greater hum that settled in behind my eyes.

Bob thought a moment, one hand kneading the other. Maybe indecision, a buzz, big notions of deception. "One hundred per cent," he said.

"I have to mention, obviously, that space travel has risks."

"I know that."

"These new launchers, they're state of the art. By Apollo standards very safe, but things go wrong."

"I know that."

I thought about my visit to the University of Minnesota's cancer centre where Bob had been treated, people in the waiting room with their clothes eight sizes too big, skin like silica dust, and the nurse saying they'd lost half their files in a cyber attack.

"Two months ago, one of this company's competitors, their launcher disintegrated on re-entry."

"Disintegrated." Bob scooped a bead of dew off his beer glass and rubbed it into his chin.

"Everyone died," I said. "Hard to know how quickly."

"And you are supposed to come with me?"

"I am obligated to come with you."

"Would they make an exception? If it's dangerous, I can go myself."

"I am obligated to come." Lies.

"Then I guess you're coming," he said, like it was his idea. He stood to play a shot, then realized the balls were all in disarray and hadn't been reracked since the previous game. With a huff he sat. Pool had ended.

"We aren't astronauts," I said. My beer had long emptied and I wanted another, but wanted to be professional. Now was not the time for one into another into another into a murky smear of hours.

"I've done some reading on space," said Bob.

We ran out of talk and sat like two almost-old men staring at the pool table. We both didn't want to play anymore. Playing made it all worse: us being there at the hall, us not being as good as we needed to be, our etched glasses, chalk-blued fingers, death on our minds. So we sat there still paying for the table but not playing. Ordered one more beer. Bob told me about his dad pushing him and his brother around in a wheelbarrow as kids. This old, rusty blue wheelbarrow, front tire half collapsed. On hot days, his dad did this without a shirt on, his wet chest sometimes pressing into Bob's back as they bounced over the trail of their property out in the sticks.

I listened and wiped my own sweat, suddenly tired, leaden-eyed. Calvin at work. A professional.

Bob began rambling more and more. Talked about moving into the city. New house. No friends. Dad puts a pool table in the basement. A bright, wooden nine-foot Brunswick with mother-of-pearl inlay on each rail. The type of table you have sex on. Would never let Bob play, though. Couldn't even touch it. Got antsy when he looked at it. But kids at high school, they somehow knew, someone had told them about the table, Bob couldn't figure out who. They'd ask him to play at the local game store open late, or at the all-ages place, or the bar that didn't card. Bob owned a table; look at Bob. Bob must be a shark. And Bob always lost.

By then Bob had the cue ball clutched in his hand, arm dangling at his side like a veiny rope. Bob's face had gone slack; no particular expression. Under this, though, roils, narcotic memory.

And he'd tell them: "My dad doesn't let me touch the table! I don't practise!" But they'd laugh it off and challenge him and gloat when they won. He'd ask his father if he could rent some time on the home table, but no. Could not even *pay* for it. Never, not a chance. Could never trust anyone.

Bob whipped his arm to the side. Cue ball through the big mirror. Glass exploded, splashed across the floor, disco knives.

A big man in a leather jacket now, looming, ready. Forehead vein a worm. Smell of black tea and armpit. What the fuck are we doing? Have we lost our minds? The floor a million tiny televisions. Bob dragged out like a duffle bag. Me, punched in the chest, stomach, arm wrenched behind my back. I half struggled. Who are these men? Who are these men?

Both of us then in the cool night. Old street and rain and caved-in cigarettes. Bob didn't say anything for fourteen seconds. We were both coughing. I checked my pockets for my wallet, phone, keys—they always got swallowed by punches. Couldn't believe he threw the pool ball. Pool balls the kind of hard object you do not throw, ever.

Bob shrugged like the whole thing was inevitable. "Fucking assholes. Could have been an accident."

I left him standing out front of the hall, and wandered to a street with cabs. Flagged one. The driver had a big silver-toothed smile. He asked about my breathing. I said, "Asthma," and he let it go and we purred off between the glossy buildings with a random spread of lit offices; I was never sure if buildings had a scheme for that: which offices stayed lit, which went dark, what the pattern was to make the building safe and scare people off like it wasn't truly empty.

I drive slow through the still-quiet streets. Bob's lips are sewn shut. One small twist of the wheel would prevent this going any further. He cranes his head forward in the car to peer at the sky, the clouds. Worry, maybe. Guilt, glee, dreams of heaven. I don't know from my seat what he's thinking. It's too late anyway. We're going regardless. Even if he confesses, we're going. Even if he swallowed a bomb for breakfast, we're going. I'll make him fucking go.

Bob goes to turn on the radio, stops halfway, retracts his hand. I flip it to FM, some soul station. Smooth bass and drums kick up from the speakers. A man sings about a girl in his glass and he'll drink her down, she's so smooth.

"Do you think it will feel like flying?" Bob asks.

"I don't know, Bob."

"Because I think it has to feel like you are suddenly really light, you know?"

"Really light," I say.

"Yeah, like you weigh nothing."

"That is the plan."

"But I think it could also feel like you've just always been so heavy and now you feel normal again."

"Is that how you feel?"

"Sometimes."

"Sometimes me too, Bob."

The launcher's civilian compartment has seats like cresting waves, rugged woven X-straps, a communication panel on the armrest, emergency information everywhere. Royal-blue theme. Blue walls, blue floor. Bob and I are next to each other in the back row. I can't really tell his expression through his helmet's faceplate, can only see his eyebrows, how they hook and show signs of grey. Everything is very shiny. Glare. Hall of mirrors.

Bob stares straight ahead, thick-suited hands in his lap.

The suit has a Halloween feel, somehow embarrasses me, is inadequate. The compartment gets hotter and hotter. Are we the fuel? Would they have told us? My breaths have gone ragged, each one chased from my mouth. Sounds of air filtration and whirring gears, robotic legs, arms, heads. There's a HUD in the helmet's glass with not quite enough information. I want to know if we are dying. I want heart rate, blood pressure, white cells. The corner of my screen shows a countdown.

Vibrations start through the soles of my boots. Deep purring. The HUD showing, *Welcome to your space flight. Everything is optimal.* Then, *We are counting down to launch.* One after another the messages come. Some about liability. *We are not liable for conflagrations.* That we are being filmed, both in the cabin and from various cameras at the launch site. We have no ownership of this footage. Family members cannot have it, even if we go down, an inferno, suits melted to steel puddles.

I'm thinking of Bob's empty house up north. The way the tiles in his kitchen looked like the sea. The job. My job. Unsent letter to corporate about Bob, my failures, my serious doubts.

The vibrations grow, a roar now. Pressure on my back, a hundred hands, a thousand.

Launch. Am I yelling? The pressure hurts and becomes so complete I feel safer than I've felt in years, cradled. My eyes pull from my head. The roar is huge, beyond anything. We move up. Up and up and up. Two Gs. Three. Five.

Clouds rip by the windows. Bob stares straight ahead. A low groan from him as we push through the atmosphere at 20,000 miles an hour. No, it's my groan. Whimpers almost. Liquid sounds pulled from my throat. A gorilla on my chest. Then sudden lightness. I pitch forward at the hips. It's too much, too sudden. Spit coats my chin, warm trails of it down my neck. A feeling of absolute stillness. It's not like falling, or rising. It's not anything. An absence.

"Oh, man. Oh, man," says Bob. "This is crazy."

"You can remove your harnesses," comes a voice over a speaker I can't see.

We cut ourselves loose. I don't know the other people, or care to. Bodies spin and glide into the false air of the compartment.

I find myself colliding with Bob, his shoulder near my face, knee to my groin, legs askew. Weird embrace. We push away from each other and bounce against the soft walls. I turn and spin, fly, flap. Most of the people gently laugh, though no one's said much. We float and rejoice and swirl our arms. Bob goes into a series of spins so fast I have to put out my arm and stop him.

"Thanks," he says.

I drift to a window. Earth below, massive curvature, blue and copper. Our poor world. I try to figure out which countries I'm looking at, which continents. It's all so small. Maybe Africa, over there Asia, New Zealand, Vietnam. Land masses eczemic with mountains.

Bob is next to me, eyes pinned open, a twitch in his cheek.

"Bob?" I say.

"This is where we are," he says and shakes his head. Trembling beads of sweat have pooled under one of his eyelids.

"Will you miss it?"

"I miss it already," he says.

"Is this what you wanted?"

"I know you weren't forced to come."

"That's okay."

"And my kitchen drawers, they don't fully close unless you lift them."

Ah.

The world has spun below us, now all ocean, Pacific, cloud skiffs. Half the world in darkness.

I watch Bob. He's turned away from me, gone very close to a window. Even without hearing him, his shudders are obvious. The back of his suit shakes and crinkles, light catching the metal weave. His shoulders curl.

I push off the wall and float behind him. Put a hand on his arm. "Bob?"

Now I can hear the breaths, the rapid huffs of not enough air. "Bob?" I say again. Bob hyperventilating. Won't look at me. No one else has noticed. I move until I'm right beside him, closer than men should get, our arms and legs touching, our hips. I throw an arm around him, feel the violent pull of his lungs. "You're okay," I say. "You're okay."

He flinches.

"It's okay. We're up here. It's okay."

For the last few minutes I stay there next to him. He soon calms, looks sidelong at me, and nods. Gives my chest a gentle tap.

Our time comes to an end. Too short. Can we go again?

We strap ourselves back in for re-entry. Bob laughs crazily now. Harnesses catch and click home. Noise builds. A corona of fire around the viewing windows, blue, red, white hot. We are America. My teeth rattle so much I bite down. This is a can ready to burst. We are recycling. They'd find us like dust in the wreckage, pour us into boxes, tell people which box represented which person so they could have special meaning. Put a name tag on the boxes so there could be no mistake.

So many before Bob. George backstage with Justin Timberlake, knew all the dances, feet gliding, pancreatic cancer. Wyatt and his African safari, Batten disease, which I'd never even heard of. Kim and her ALS, our Tibetan getaway with the monks, two thin mattresses on the stone floor. Kim above all. Kim, who cut her hair to be more streamlined, like death had friction and she could get through faster, sleek, and unnoticed. Who one time told me *I* would be okay. Give her all the wishes, a new body, head transplant, upload to the cloud, her digital hair ten feet long, fifty feet, a sail. And all the files in the rental house, more people on the cusp, even as we rocket down, the urgency of them, application paper almost hot and splotched by soup and tears and the oil of a trembling finger; I'd slept on the pages, tasted them, woke with them stuck to me like strange garments.

We punch into atmosphere, the wall of it. Clay, sheet metal, bricks. The Gs climb and build on my shoulders. I am multiplied. I would be okay. I would be okay.

We are immense, dripping wet, pinned to the seats. A needle through the bright cloth sky. Aflame. They are all watching us, the people below with their cameras. Streaking over the oceans now. Follicle reefs, seed islands. Roar of air and metal. Can't move our heads, or blink or feel our stomachs drop. No individual parts remain. Limbless and soft and one round piece: we must hold still. Must focus and wait for instruction. Bird in our ear. Hidden speaker. What to do. Where. How. Ejection and parachutes. And we would do that. Do anything. Twirl knobs, livestream, scrawl goodbyes in window fog. Be still. Plunge, and never ever look away.

ABOUT THE CONTRIBUTORS

Sarah Christina Brown's writing has appeared in *PRISM international*, *The Dalhousie Review*, *Room*, *EVENT*, and *Cosmonauts Avenue*. She was shortlisted for 2018's RBC Bronwen Wallace Award for Emerging Writers. She works as an English instructor in New Westminster, B.C., where she is completing a collection of short fiction.

Kai Conradi is a queer and trans poet and short story writer from Cumberland, B.C. He is currently finishing an undergraduate degree in writing at the University of Victoria. Kai's work has appeared in *Poetry*, *The Malahat Review*, and *Grain*, and has been nominated for the Pushcart Prize and the National Magazine Awards. "Every True Artist" is his first published story and also appears in *Best Canadian Stories 2019*.

Francesca Ekwuyasi is a writer and filmmaker from Lagos, Nigeria. Her work explores themes of faith, family, queerness, consumption, loneliness, and belonging. Her writing has been published in *Winter Tangerine*, *Brittle Paper*, *Transition Magazine*, *The Malahat Review*, *Visual Arts News*, *Sitelines* for Eyelevel Gallery, and *GUTS*, and elsewhere. She wrote collaboratively for Heist Theatre's show *Frequencies*, and her short documentary *Black + Belonging* premiered at the Halifax Black Film Festival. Francesca is currently at work on a film project that navigates the intersections of queerness and faith. Find more of her work at ekwuyasi.com.

Jason Jobin grew up on an acreage in a Yukon forest. He completed a B.A. and M.F.A. in writing at the University of Victoria, where he studied fiction and screenwriting, and developed his own course on how to rap. His fiction has won *The Malahat Review*'s Jack Hodgins Founders' Award and a Silver at the National Magazine Awards, and has been long-listed for *The Fiddlehead* Prize. For him, writing is a place to show the fallout of people in suddenly new situations, the moments that wake you up and that you think back on when falling asleep. He currently lives and writes in Victoria and is working on a short story collection and novel.

Hajera Khaja's fiction has been published in *Joyland*, and her writing has appeared in the *National Post* and *Ottawa Citizen*. "Waiting for Adnan" is her first fiction publication. She lives in Mississauga, Ontario, and is presently working on putting together a short story collection.

Ben Ladouceur is the author of *Mad Long Emotion*, a poetry collection published by Coach House Books in 2019. His first poetry collection, *Otter* (Coach House Books), was selected as a best book of 2015 by the *National Post*, nominated for a Lambda Literary Award, and awarded the 2016 Gerald Lampert Memorial Award for best debut collection in Canada. He received the 2018 Writers' Trust Dayne Ogilvie Prize for emerging LGBTQ writers. He lives in Ottawa.

Angélique Lalonde grew up in Ktunaxa Territory. Her mother is Métis and her father is Québécois. The stories she has about her ancestors have a lot of knots in them. She writes, grows

food, harvests medicines, and works as a community organizer on Gitxsan Territory, where she lives as an uninvited
guest with her children, partner, and many non-human beings.
Angélique holds a Ph.D. in anthropology from the University
of Victoria. In 2018, her story "Pooka" was runner up for
PRISM international's Jacob Zilber Prize for Short Fiction.
She is currently at work on a collection of short stories.

Michael LaPointe has written for *The Atlantic* and *The New
Yorker*, and he is a columnist with *The Paris Review*. His work
has been collected in *Best Canadian Stories* and nominated for
the National Magazine Awards, and his debut novel, *The Creep*,
will be published by Random House Canada in Spring 2021.

Canisia Lubrin is a writer, editor, and teacher. Her work has
been published widely and frequently anthologized, including translations into Spanish. She has been nominated for the
Toronto Book Award, Gerald Lampert Award, Pat Lowther
Award, and others. The story "No ID or We Could Be Brothers" has been translated into Italian and is included in *Code
Noir*, her in-progress collection of linked short stories. She is
the author of the poetry collection *Voodoo Hypothesis* (Buckrider
Books/Wolsak & Wynn, 2017), which was named a CBC Best
Book, and *The Dyzgraphist* (McClelland & Stewart, 2020). She
holds an M.F.A. from the University of Guelph.

Samantha Jade Macpherson is a writer from the Okanagan
Valley and an M.F.A. fiction candidate at the Iowa Writers'
Workshop. Her work has been published in *The Fiddlehead*, *The
Malahat Review*, and *Ricepaper Magazine*. Her story "Tattoo"

was the winner of *The Malahat Review*'s 2018 Novella Prize, as well as the Jack Hodgins Founders' Award for Fiction. She holds a degree in creative writing from the University of Victoria and is currently at work on a collection of linked stories.

Troy Sebastian / nupqu ʔak·ɫaṁ is a Ktunaxa writer from ʔaq̓am. He completed the Banff Centre's Indigenous Writers program and is an M.F.A. student at the University of Victoria's writing program. His work has been published in *The Walrus*, *Ktuqeǂakyam*, *The Malahat Review*, *The New Quarterly*, *Quill & Quire*, and *Prairie Fire*. He was shortlisted for *Briarpatch*'s 2016 Writing in the Margins contest, was a recipient of the 2017 Hnatyshyn Foundation's REVEAL Indigenous Art Award, and longlisted for CBC's 2018 Short Story Prize.

Diagnosed with bipolar disorder at seventeen, **Leanne Toshiko Simpson** writes about navigating Scarborough's psychiatric system armed with the love of her obachan and her trusty anxiety raccoon. Her stories have appeared in *Matrix Magazine*, *Release Any Words Stuck Inside of You: An untethered Collection of Shorts*, and *The Unpublished City, Volume II*. She is a spokesperson for Bell Let's Talk and was named Scarborough's 2016 Emerging Writer. In her spare time, Leanne teaches creative writing at the Centre for Addiction and Mental Health and InkWell Workshops. She is currently completing a mental health–centred novel for her M.F.A. at the University of Guelph.

For more information about the publications that submitted to this year's competition, The Journey Prize, and *The Journey Prize Stories*, please visit www.facebook.com/TheJourneyPrize.

Brick is an international literary journal published twice a year out of Toronto. With a focus on literary non-fiction—and a willingness to stray when our hearts are taken—the magazine prizes the personal voice and is guided by the following words from Rainer Maria Rilke: "Works of art are of an infinite loneliness and with nothing to be so little reached as with criticism. Only love can grasp and hold and fairly judge them." We seek writing on anything that obsesses writers, fuels their practice, invigorates their imaginations, and imbues them with awe. *Brick*'s role is to showcase Canadian and Turtle Island writers in an international context and connect them with a global audience, and we welcome diverse voices charting broad imaginings, current conversations, rich ideas, urgent passions, and beautiful, thoughtful, difficult, or irreverent art. *Brick* was established in 1977 in London, Ontario, by Stan Dragland and Jean McKay, and is now edited by Dionne Brand, David Chariandy, Laurie D. Graham, Michael Helm, Liz Johnston, Martha Sharpe, Rebecca Silver Slayter, and Madeleine Thien. Publisher: Laurie D. Graham. Managing Editor: Allison LaSorda. Submissions and correspondence: *Brick, A Literary Journal*, Box 609, Stn. P, Toronto, ON, M5S 2Y4. Website: brickmag.com

EVENT has inspired and nurtured writers for almost five decades. Featuring the very best in contemporary writing from Canada and abroad, *EVENT* consistently publishes award-winning fiction, poetry, non-fiction, notes on writing, and critical reviews—all topped off by stunning Canadian cover art and illustrations. Stories first published in *EVENT* regularly appear in the *Best Canadian Stories* and *Journey Prize Stories* anthologies, are finalists at the National Magazine Awards, and recently won the Grand Prix Best Literature and Art Story at the 2017 Canadian Magazine Awards. *EVENT* is also home to Canada's longest-running non-fiction contest (fall deadline), and its Reading Service for Writers. Editor: Shashi Bhat. Managing Editor: Ian Cockfield. Fiction Editor: Christine Dewar. Correspondence: *EVENT*, P.O. Box 2503, New Westminster, BC, V3L 5B2. Email (queries only): event@douglascollege.ca Website: www.eventmagazine.ca

The Fiddlehead, Atlantic Canada's longest-running literary journal, publishes short fiction, poetry, creative non-fiction, and book reviews. It appears four times a year and sponsors three contests (in short fiction, poetry, and creative non-fiction) that award a total of $6,000 in prizes. *The Fiddlehead* is open to good writing in English or translations into English from all over the world and in a variety of styles, including experimental genres. Editor: Sue Sinclair. Submissions and correspondence: *The Fiddlehead*, Campus House, 11 Garland Court, University of New Brunswick, P.O. Box 4400, Fredericton, NB, E3B 5A3. Email (queries only): fiddlehd@unb.ca Website: www.thefiddlehead.ca Twitter: @TheFiddlehd. You can also find *The Fiddlehead* on Facebook.

GUTS is a digital, volunteer-run feminist publication that aims to further feminist discourse, criticism, and community engagement in Canada. Encouraged and inspired by the wide range of thought and experience that exists within the young Canadian feminist movement, *GUTS* wants to shed some much-needed light on the systemic forces and intersecting oppressions that isolate women, non-binary, and trans people across the country. Through the collective interpretation of feminist issues, *GUTS* strives to create a public for a new kind of correspondence. Founding Editors: Nadine Adelaar and Cynthia Spring. Managing Editor: Brett Cassady Willes. Senior Editor: Natalie Childs. Editors: Katie Lew and Carmina Ravanera. Poetry Editor: Tess Liem. Communications and Engagement Manager: Celia Zhang. Website: gutsmagazine.ca

Based on the idea that fiction is an international movement supported by local communities, **Joyland** is a literary magazine that selects stories regionally. Our editors work with authors connected to locales across North America, including New York, Los Angeles, and Toronto, as well as places underrepresented in cultural media. Our ten regional verticals highlight the diversity of voices nationwide, and we are proud to have created a home where all can coexist. Publisher and Editorial Director: Kyle Lucia Wu. Executive Editor: Michelle Lyn King. Section Editors: Amy Shearn, Lisa Locascio, Kate Folk, Kathryn Mockler, Rachel Morgenstern-Clarren, Bryan Hurt, Michelle Lyn King, Laura Chow Reeve, and Kait Heacock.

The Malahat Review is a quarterly journal of contemporary poetry, fiction, and creative non-fiction by emerging and established writers from Canada and abroad. Summer issues feature the winners of the magazine's Novella and Long Poem prizes, held in alternating years; the fall issues feature the winners of the Far Horizons Award for emerging writers, alternating between poetry and fiction each year; the winter issues feature the winners of the Constance Rooke Creative Non-fiction Prize; and the spring issues feature winners of the Open Season Awards in all three genres (poetry, fiction, and creative non-fiction). All issues feature covers by noted Canadian visual artists and include reviews of Canadian books. Editor: Iain Higgins. Assistant Editor: Rhonda Batchelor. Correspondence: *The Malahat Review*, University of Victoria, P.O. Box 1800, Station CSC, Victoria, BC, V8W 3H5. Unsolicited submissions and contest entries are accepted through Submittable only (review contest guidelines before entering). Email: malahat@uvic.ca Website: www.malahatreview.ca Twitter: @malahatreview Facebook: The-Malahat-Review Instagram: malahatreview

PRISM international is a quarterly magazine out of Vancouver, B.C., whose office is located on the traditional, ancestral, and unceded territory of the xʷməθkʷəy̓əm people. Our mandate is to publish the best in contemporary writing and translation from Canada and around the world. Writing from *PRISM* has been featured in *Best American Stories*, *Best American Essays*, and *The Journey Prize Stories*, among other noted publications. *PRISM* strives to uplift and shine a light on emerging and established voices across Canada and internationally, and is especially committed to providing a platform for folks who have been systematically marginalized in the literary community, including but not limited to BIPOC groups, cis women, trans women and men, non-binary people, people with disabilities, and members of the LGBTQ2S community. Content Editors: Molly Cross-Blanchard and Emma Cleary. Executive Editors: Shristi Uprety and Kate Black. Reviews Editor: Cara Nelissen. Submissions and Correspondence: *PRISM international* Creative Writing Program, UBC Buch. E462—1866 Main Mall Vancouver, BC, V6T 1Z1 Website: www.prismmagazine.ca

Release Any Words Stuck Inside of You is an annual anthology of Canadian short prose published by Applebeard Editions. It features writing from some of the most established authors in Canada, such as Lorna Crozier, George Elliott Clarke, and Priscila Uppal, alongside some of the newest. Prose poems, flash fiction, questionnaires, rants, letters . . . no topic or form is off limits as long as it's short (750 words or less) and doesn't contain any line breaks. Edited by Nicole Haldoupis and Geoff Pevlin. Follow them on social media @ApplebeardBooks, and read samples on the website or contribute to this year's edition at www.applebeardeditions.ca.

The Walrus is a national general interest magazine about Canada and its place in the world. We are committed to presenting the best art and writing, including works of poetry and fiction, from Canada and elsewhere, on a wide range of topics for curious readers. Executive Director and Publisher: Shelley Ambrose. Editorial: Jessica Johnson, Carmine Starnino,

Samia Madwar, Hamutal Dotan, Lauren McKeon, Harley Rustad, Daniel Viola, Viviane Fairbank, and Erin Sylvester. Correspondence: *The Walrus*, PO Box 915, Stn. Main, Markham, ON, L3P 0A8. Website: www.thewalrus.ca

Submissions were also received from the following publications:

Agnes and True
(Toronto, ON)
www.agnesandtrue.com

Augur Magazine
www.augurmag.com

Blank Spaces
blankspaces.alannarusnak.com

carte blanche
(Montreal, QC)
www.carte-blanche.org

The Dalhousie Review
dalhousiereview.dal.ca

Don't Talk to Me About Love
(Toronto, ON)
www.donttalktomeabout
love.org

Glass Buffalo
(Edmonton, AB)
www.glassbuffalo.com

Grain
(Saskatoon, SK)
www.grainmagazine.ca

The Humber Literary Review
(Toronto, ON)
www.humberliteraryreview.
com

Little Fiction | Big Truths
(Toronto, ON)
www.littlefiction.com

The New Quarterly
www.tnq.ca

On Spec
(Edmonton, AB)
www.onspec.ca

Plenitude Magazine
(Victoria, BC)
www.plenitudemagazine.ca

Portal Magazine
www.portalmagazine.ca

Prairie Fire
(Winnipeg, MB)
www.prairiefire.ca

The Prairie Journal
(Calgary, AB)
www.prairiejournal.org

Pulp Literature
(Richmond, BC)
www.pulpliterature.com

The Puritan
(Toronto, ON)
www.puritanmagazine.com

Queen's Quarterly
(Kingston, ON)
www.queensu.ca/quarterly

Riddle Fence
(St. John's, NL)
www.riddlefence.com

Room Magazine
(Vancouver, BC)
www.roommagazine.com

Shades Within Us
laksamedia.com

subTerrain Magazine
(Vancouver, BC)
www.subterrain.ca

Taddle Creek
(Toronto, ON)
www.taddlecreekmag.com

The /tɛmz/ Review
(London, ON)
www.thetemzreview.com

The Unexpected Sky
www.inkwellworkshops.com

University of Toronto Magazine
magazine.utoronto.ca

untethered
(Toronto, ON)
www.alwaysuntethered.com

PREVIOUS CONTRIBUTING AUTHORS

* Winners of the $10,000 Journey Prize
** Co-winners of the $10,000 Journey Prize

1

1989

SELECTED WITH ALISTAIR MacLEOD

Ven Begamudré, "Word Games"
David Bergen, "Where You're From"
Lois Braun, "The Pumpkin-Eaters"
Constance Buchanan, "Man with Flying Genitals"
Ann Copeland, "Obedience"
Marion Douglas, "Flags"
Frances Itani, "An Evening in the Café"
Diane Keating, "The Crying Out"
Thomas King, "One Good Story, That One"
Holley Rubinsky, "Rapid Transits"*
Jean Rysstad, "Winter Baby"
Kevin Van Tighem, "Whoopers"
M.G. Vassanji, "In the Quiet of a Sunday Afternoon"
Bronwen Wallace, "Chicken 'N' Ribs"
Armin Wiebe, "Mouse Lake"
Budge Wilson, "Waiting"

2

1990

SELECTED WITH LEON ROOKE; GUY VANDERHAEGHE

André Alexis, "Despair: Five Stories of Ottawa"
Glen Allen, "The Hua Guofeng Memorial Warehouse"
Marusia Bociurkiw, "Mama, Donya"
Virgil Burnett, "Billfrith the Dreamer"
Margaret Dyment, "Sacred Trust"
Cynthia Flood, "My Father Took a Cake to France"*
Douglas Glover, "Story Carved in Stone"
Terry Griggs, "Man with the Axe"
Rick Hillis, "Limbo River"

Thomas King, "The Dog I Wish I Had, I Would Call It Helen"
K.D. Miller, "Sunrise Till Dark"
Jennifer Mitton, "Let Them Say"
Lawrence O'Toole, "Goin' to Town with Katie Ann"
Kenneth Radu, "A Change of Heart"
Jenifer Sutherland, "Table Talk"
Wayne Tefs, "Red Rock and After"

3
1991
SELECTED WITH JANE URQUHART

Donald Aker, "The Invitation"
Anton Baer, "Yukon"
Allan Barr, "A Visit from Lloyd"
David Bergen, "The Fall"
Rai Berzins, "Common Sense"
Diana Hartog, "Theories of Grief"
Diane Keating, "The Salem Letters"
Yann Martel, "The Facts Behind the Helsinki Roccamatios"*
Jennifer Mitton, "Polaroid"
Sheldon Oberman, "This Business with Elijah"
Lynn Podgurny, "Till Tomorrow, Maple Leaf Mills"
James Riseborough, "She Is Not His Mother"
Patricia Stone, "Living on the Lake"

4
1992
SELECTED WITH SANDRA BIRDSELL

David Bergen, "The Bottom of the Glass"
Maria A. Billion, "No Miracles Sweet Jesus"
Judith Cowan, "By the Big River"
Steven Heighton, "How Beautiful upon the Mountains"
Steven Heighton, "A Man Away from Home Has No Neighbours"
L. Rex Kay, "Travelling"
Rozena Maart, "No Rosa, No District Six"*
Guy Malet De Carteret, "Rainy Day"
Carmelita McGrath, "Silence"
Michael Mirolla, "A Theory of Discontinuous Existence"
Diane Juttner Perreault, "Bella's Story"
Eden Robinson, "Traplines"

5
1993
SELECTED WITH GUY VANDERHAEGHE

Caroline Adderson, "Oil and Dread"
David Bergen, "La Rue Prevette"
Marina Endicott, "With the Band"
Dayv James-French, "Cervine"
Michael Kenyon, "Durable Tumblers"
K.D. Miller, "A Litany in Time of Plague"
Robert Mullen, "Flotsam"
Gayla Reid, "Sister Doyle's Men"*
Oakland Ross, "Bang-bang"
Robert Sherrin, "Technical Battle for Trial Machine"
Carol Windley, "The Etruscans"

6
1994
SELECTED WITH DOUGLAS GLOVER;
JUDITH CHANT (CHAPTERS)

Anne Carson, "Water Margins: An Essay on Swimming by My Brother"
Richard Cumyn, "The Sound He Made"
Genni Gunn, "Versions"
Melissa Hardy, "Long Man the River"*
Robert Mullen, "Anomie"
Vivian Payne, "Free Falls"
Jim Reil, "Dry"
Robyn Sarah, "Accept My Story"
Joan Skogan, "Landfall"
Dorothy Speak, "Relatives in Florida"
Alison Wearing, "Notes from Under Water"

7
1995
SELECTED WITH M.G. VASSANJI;
RICHARD BACHMANN (A DIFFERENT DRUMMER BOOKS)

Michelle Alfano, "Opera"
Mary Borsky, "Maps of the Known World"
Gabriella Goliger, "Song of Ascent"
Elizabeth Hay, "Hand Games"
Shaena Lambert, "The Falling Woman"
Elise Levine, "Boy"

Roger Burford Mason, "The Rat-Catcher's Kiss"
Antanas Sileika, "Going Native"
Kathryn Woodward, "Of Marranos and Gilded Angels"*

8
1996
SELECTED WITH OLIVE SENIOR;
BEN MCNALLY (NICHOLAS HOARE LTD.)

Rick Bowers, "Dental Bytes"
David Elias, "How I Crossed Over"
Elyse Gasco, "Can You Wave Bye Bye, Baby?"*
Danuta Gleed, "Bones"
Elizabeth Hay, "The Friend"
Linda Holeman, "Turning the Worm"
Elaine Littman, "The Winner's Circle"
Murray Logan, "Steam"
Rick Maddocks, "Lessons from the Sputnik Diner"
K.D. Miller, "Egypt Land"
Gregor Robinson, "Monster Gaps"
Alma Subasic, "Dust"

9
1997
SELECTED WITH NINO RICCI; NICHOLAS PASHLEY
(UNIVERSITY OF TORONTO BOOKSTORE)

Brian Bartlett, "Thomas, Naked"
Dennis Bock, "Olympia"
Kristen den Hartog, "Wave"
Gabriella Goliger, "Maladies of the Inner Ear"**
Terry Griggs, "Momma Had a Baby"
Mark Anthony Jarman, "Righteous Speedboat"
Judith Kalman, "Not for Me a Crown of Thorns"
Andrew Mullins, "The World of Science"
Sasenarine Persaud, "Canada Geese and Apple Chatney"
Anne Simpson, "Dreaming Snow"**
Sarah Withrow, "Ollie"
Terence Young, "The Berlin Wall"

10
1998

SELECTED BY PETER BUITENHUIS; HOLLEY RUBINSKY;
CELIA DUTHIE (DUTHIE BOOKS LTD.)

John Brooke, "The Finer Points of Apples"*

Ian Colford, "The Reason for the Dream"

Libby Creelman, "Cruelty"

Michael Crummey, "Serendipity"

Stephen Guppy, "Downwind"

Jane Eaton Hamilton, "Graduation"

Elise Levine, "You Are You Because Your Little Dog Loves You"

Jean McNeil, "Bethlehem"

Liz Moore, "Eight-Day Clock"

Edward O'Connor, "The Beatrice of Victoria College"

Tim Rogers, "Scars and Other Presents"

Denise Ryan, "Marginals, Vivisections, and Dreams"

Madeleine Thien, "Simple Recipes"

Cheryl Tibbetts, "Flowers of Africville"

11
1999

SELECTED BY LESLEY CHOYCE; SHELDON CURRIE;
MARY-JO ANDERSON (FROG HOLLOW BOOKS)

Mike Barnes, "In Florida"

Libby Creelman, "Sunken Island"

Mike Finigan, "Passion Sunday"

Jane Eaton Hamilton, "Territory"

Mark Anthony Jarman, "Travels into Several Remote Nations of the World"

Barbara Lambert, "Where the Bodies Are Kept"

Linda Little, "The Still"

Larry Lynch, "The Sitter"

Sandra Sabatini, "The One with the News"

Sharon Steams, "Brothers"

Mary Walters, "Show Jumping"

Alissa York, "The Back of the Bear's Mouth"*

12

2000

SELECTED BY CATHERINE BUSH; HAL NIEDZVIECKI; MARC GLASSMAN (PAGES BOOKS AND MAGAZINES)

Andrew Gray, "The Heart of the Land"

Lee Henderson, "Sheep Dub"

Jessica Johnson, "We Move Slowly"

John Lavery, "The Premier's New Pyjamas"

J.A. McCormack, "Hearsay"

Nancy Richler, "Your Mouth Is Lovely"

Andrew Smith, "Sightseeing"

Karen Solie, "Onion Calendar"

Timothy Taylor, "Doves of Townsend"*

Timothy Taylor, "Pope's Own"

Timothy Taylor, "Silent Cruise"

R.M. Vaughan, "Swan Street"

13

2001

SELECTED BY ELYSE GASCO; MICHAEL HELM; MICHAEL NICHOLSON (INDIGO BOOKS & MUSIC INC.)

Kevin Armstrong, "The Cane Field"*

Mike Barnes, "Karaoke Mon Amour"

Heather Birrell, "Machaya"

Heather Birrell, "The Present Perfect"

Craig Boyko, "The Gun"

Vivette J. Kady, "Anything That Wiggles"

Billie Livingston, "You're Taking All the Fun Out of It"

Annabel Lyon, "Fishes"

Lisa Moore, "The Way the Light Is"

Heather O'Neill, "Little Suitcase"

Susan Rendell, "In the Chambers of the Sea"

Tim Rogers, "Watch"

Margrith Schraner, "Dream Dig"

14
2002
SELECTED BY ANDRÉ ALEXIS;
DEREK McCORMACK; DIANE SCHOEMPERLEN

Mike Barnes, "Cogagwee"

Geoffrey Brown, "Listen"

Jocelyn Brown, "Miss Canada"*

Emma Donoghue, "What Remains"

Jonathan Goldstein, "You Are a Spaceman with Your Head Under the
    Bathroom Stall Door"

Robert McGill, "Confidence Men"

Robert McGill, "The Stars Are Falling"

Nick Melling, "Philemon"

Robert Mullen, "Alex the God"

Karen Munro, "The Pool"

Leah Postman, "Being Famous"

Neil Smith, "Green Fluorescent Protein"

15
2003
SELECTED BY MICHELLE BERRY;
TIMOTHY TAYLOR; MICHAEL WINTER

Rosaria Campbell, "Reaching"

Hilary Dean, "The Lemon Stories"

Dawn Rae Downton, "Hansel and Gretel"

Anne Fleming, "Gay Dwarves of America"

Elyse Friedman, "Truth"

Charlotte Gill, "Hush"

Jessica Grant, "My Husband's Jump"*

Jacqueline Honnet, "Conversion Classes"

S.K. Johannesen, "Resurrection"

Avner Mandelman, "Cuckoo"

Tim Mitchell, "Night Finds Us"

Heather O'Neill, "The Difference Between Me and Goldstein"

16

2004

SELECTED BY ELIZABETH HAY; LISA MOORE; MICHAEL REDHILL

Anar Ali, "Baby Khaki's Wings"

Kenneth Bonert, "Packers and Movers"

Jennifer Clouter, "Benny and the Jets"

Daniel Griffin, "Mercedes Buyer's Guide"

Michael Kissinger, "Invest in the North"

Devin Krukoff, "The Last Spark"*

Elaine McCluskey, "The Watermelon Social"

William Metcalfe, "Nice Big Car, Rap Music Coming Out the Window"

Lesley Millard, "The Uses of the Neckerchief"

Adam Lewis Schroeder, "Burning the Cattle at Both Ends"

Michael V. Smith, "What We Wanted"

Neil Smith, "Isolettes"

Patricia Rose Young, "Up the Clyde on a Bike"

17

2005

SELECTED BY JAMES GRAINGER AND NANCY LEE

Randy Boyagoda, "Rice and Curry Yacht Club"

Krista Bridge, "A Matter of Firsts"

Josh Byer, "Rats, Homosex, Saunas, and Simon"

Craig Davidson, "Failure to Thrive"

McKinley M. Hellenes, "Brighter Thread"

Catherine Kidd, "Green-Eyed Beans"

Pasha Malla, "The Past Composed"

Edward O'Connor, "Heard Melodies Are Sweet"

Barbara Romanik, "Seven Ways into Chandigarh"

Sandra Sabatini, "The Dolphins at Sainte Marie"

Matt Shaw, "Matchbook for a Mother's Hair"*

Richard Simas, "Anthropologies"

Neil Smith, "Scrapbook"

Emily White, "Various Metals"

18
2006
SELECTED BY STEVEN GALLOWAY; ZSUZSI GARTNER; ANNABEL LYON

Heather Birrell, "BriannaSusannaAlana"*
Craig Boyko, "The Baby"
Craig Boyko, "The Beloved Departed"
Nadia Bozak, "Heavy Metal Housekeeping"
Lee Henderson, "Conjugation"
Melanie Little, "Wrestling"
Matthew Rader, "The Lonesome Death of Joseph Fey"
Scott Randall, "Law School"
Sarah Selecky, "Throwing Cotton"
Damian Tarnopolsky, "Sleepy"
Martin West, "Cretacea"
David Whitton, "The Eclipse"
Clea Young, "Split"

19
2007
SELECTED BY CAROLINE ADDERSON; DAVID BEZMOZGIS; DIONNE BRAND

Andrew J. Borkowski, "Twelve Versions of Lech"
Craig Boyko, "OZY"*
Grant Buday, "The Curve of the Earth"
Nicole Dixon, "High-Water Mark"
Krista Foss, "Swimming in Zanzibar"
Pasha Malla, "Respite"
Alice Petersen, "After Summer"
Patricia Robertson, "My Hungarian Sister"
Rebecca Rosenblum, "Chilly Girl"
Nicholas Ruddock, "How Eunice Got Her Baby"
Jean Van Loon, "Stardust"

20
2008
SELECTED BY LYNN COADY; HEATHER O'NEILL; NEIL SMITH
Théodora Armstrong, "Whale Stories"
Mike Christie, "Goodbye Porkpie Hat"
Anna Leventhal, "The Polar Bear at the Museum"
Naomi K. Lewis, "The Guiding Light"
Oscar Martens, "Breaking on the Wheel"
Dana Mills, "Steaming for Godthab"
Saleema Nawaz, "My Three Girls"*
Scott Randall, "The Gifted Class"
S. Kennedy Sobol, "Some Light Down"
Sarah Steinberg, "At Last at Sea"
Clea Young, "Chaperone"

21
2009
SELECTED BY CAMILLA GIBB;
LEE HENDERSON; REBECCA ROSENBLUM
Daniel Griffin, "The Last Great Works of Alvin Cale"
Jesus Hardwell, "Easy Living"
Paul Headrick, "Highlife"
Sarah Keevil, "Pyro"
Adrian Michael Kelly, "Lure"
Fran Kimmel, "Picturing God's Ocean"
Lynne Kutsukake, "Away"
Alexander MacLeod, "Miracle Mile"
Dave Margoshes, "The Wisdom of Solomon"
Shawn Syms, "On the Line"
Sarah L. Taggart, "Deaf"
Yasuko Thanh, "Floating Like the Dead"*

22
2010
SELECTED BY PASHA MALLA; JOAN THOMAS; ALISSA YORK

Carolyn Black, "Serial Love"
Andrew Boden, "Confluence of Spoors"
Laura Boudreau, "The Dead Dad Game"
Devon Code, "Uncle Oscar"*
Danielle Egan, "Publicity"
Krista Foss, "The Longitude of Okay"
Lynne Kutsukake, "Mating"
Ben Lof, "When in the Field with Her at His Back"
Andrew MacDonald, "Eat Fist!"
Eliza Robertson, "Ship's Log"
Mike Spry, "Five Pounds Short and Apologies to Nelson Algren"
Damian Tarnopolsky, "Laud We the Gods"

23
2011
SELECTED BY ALEXANDER MacLEOD;
ALISON PICK; SARAH SELECKY

Jay Brown, "The Girl from the War"
Michael Christie, "The Extra"
Seyward Goodhand, "The Fur Trader's Daughter"
Miranda Hill, "Petitions to Saint Chronic"*
Fran Kimmel, "Laundry Day"
Ross Klatte, "First-Calf Heifer"
Michelle Serwatuk, "My Eyes Are Dim"
Jessica Westhead, "What I Would Say"
Michelle Winters, "Toupée"
D.W. Wilson, "The Dead Roads"

24
2012
SELECTED BY MICHAEL CHRISTIE;
KATHRYN KUITENBROUWER; KATHLEEN WINTER

Kris Bertin, "Is Alive and Can Move"
Shashi Bhat, "Why I Read *Beowulf*"
Astrid Blodgett, "Ice Break"
Trevor Corkum, "You Were Loved"
Nancy Jo Cullen, "Ashes"
Kevin Hardcastle, "To Have to Wait"
Andrew Hood, "I'm Sorry and Thank You"
Andrew Hood, "Manning"
Grace O'Connell, "The Many Faces of Montgomery Clift"
Jasmina Odor, "Barcelona"
Alex Pugsley, "Crisis on Earth-X"*
Eliza Robertson, "Sea Drift"
Martin West, "My Daughter of the Dead Reeds"

25
2013
SELECTED BY MIRANDA HILL;
MARK MEDLEY; RUSSELL WANGERSKY

Steven Benstead, "Megan's Bus"
Jay Brown, "The Egyptians"
Andrew Forbes, "In the Foothills"
Philip Huynh, "Gulliver's Wife"
Amy Jones, "Team Ninja"
Marnie Lamb, "Mrs. Fujimoto's Wednesday Afternoons"
Doretta Lau, "How Does a Single Blade of Grass Thank the Sun?"
Laura Legge, "It's Raining in Paris"
Natalie Morrill, "Ossicles"
Zoey Leigh Peterson, "Sleep World"
Eliza Robertson, "My Sister Sang"
Naben Ruthnum, "Cinema Rex"*

26
2014
SELECTED BY STEVEN W. BEATTIE;
CRAIG DAVIDSON; SALEEMA NAWAZ

Rosaria Campbell, "Probabilities"

Nancy Jo Cullen, "Hashtag Maggie Vandermeer"

M.A. Fox, "Piano Boy"

Kevin Hardcastle, "Old Man Marchuk"

Amy Jones, "Wolves, Cigarettes, Gum"

Tyler Keevil, "Sealskin"*

Jeremy Lanaway, "Downturn"

Andrew MacDonald, "Four Minutes"

Lori McNulty, "Monsoon Season"

Shana Myara, "Remainders"

Julie Roorda, "How to Tell If Your Frog Is Dead"

Leona Theis, "High Beams"

Clea Young, "Juvenile"

27
2015
SELECTED BY ANTHONY DE SA,
TANIS RIDEOUT, AND CARRIE SNYDER

Charlotte Bondy, "Renaude"

Emily Bossé, "Last Animal Standing on Gentleman's Farm"

Deirdre Dore, "The Wise Baby"*

Charlie Fiset, "Maggie's Farm"

K'ari Fisher, "Mercy Beatrice Wrestles the Noose"

Anna Ling Kaye, "Red Egg and Ginger"

Andrew MacDonald, "The Perfect Man for My Husband"

Madeleine Maillet, "Achilles' Death"

Lori McNulty, "Fingernecklace"

Sarah Meehan Sirk, "Moonman"

Ron Schafrick, "Lovely Company"

Georgia Wilder, "Cocoa Divine and the Lightning Police"

28
2016
SELECTED BY KATE CAYLEY;
BRIAN FRANCIS; MADELEINE THIEN

Carleigh Baker, "Chins and Elbows"

Paige Cooper, "The Roar"

Charlie Fiset, "If I Ever See the Sun"

Mahak Jain, "The Origin of Jaanvi"

Colette Langlois, "The Emigrants"*

Alex Leslie, "The Person You Want to See"

Andrew MacDonald, "Progress on a Genetic Level"

J.R. McConvey, "Home Range"

J.R. McConvey, "How the Grizzly Came to Hang in the Royal Oak Hotel"

Souvankham Thammavongsa, "Mani Pedi"

Souvankham Thammavongsa, "Paris"

29
2017
SELECTED BY KEVIN HARDCASTLE;
GRACE O'CONNELL; AYELET TSABARI

Lisa Alward, "Old Growth"

Sharon Bala, "Butter Tea at Starbucks"*

Sharon Bala, "Reading Week"

Patrick Doerksen, "Leech"

Sarah Kabamba, "They Come Crying

Michael Meagher, "Used to It"

Darlene Naponse, "She Is Water"

Maria Reva, "Subject Winifred"

Jack Wang, "The Nature of Things"

Kelly Ward, "A Girl and a Dog on a Friday Night"

30
2018

SELECTED BY SHARON BALA;
KERRY CLARE; ZOEY LEIGH PETERSON

Shashi Bhat, "Mute"*

Greg Brown, "Bear"

Greg Brown, "Love"

Alicia Elliott, "Tracks"

Liz Harmer, "Never Prosper"

Philip Huynh, "The Forbidden Purple City"

Jason Jobin, "Before He Left"

Aviva Dale Martin, "Barcelona"

Rowan McCandless, "Castaways"

Sofia Mostaghimi, "Desperada"

Jess Taylor, "Two Sex Addicts Fall in Love"

Iryn Tushabe, "A Separation"

Carly Vandergriendt, "Resurfacing"